Deciding Fate

Tamra Lassiter

www.tamra.lassiter.com

Deciding Fate

Tamra Lassiter

This is a work of fiction. Certain real locations are mentioned, however all names, characters, events and incidents described in this book are fictitious or a product of the author's imagination. Any resemblance to real persons, living or deceased, is entirely coincidental.

www.tamralassiter.com

For Trinh

Chapter One

Kate

I didn't sign up for this.

An airplane, a bus, a car that slid off the road, and now I'm walking. In a snowstorm. *Definitely not what I planned when I woke up this morning.*

Sleet pelts my already tender cheeks. They're practically raw, but my feet—they may never be the same. Stabbing pain with every step I take, but every one gets me closer to the cabin.

Almost there.

Just put one foot in front of the other. The tune pops into my head from a distant childhood memory. Was it *Frosty the Snowman*? The cheery song doesn't fit my current situation. Whoever wrote that song wasn't talking about walking uphill —no, more like trudging uphill to avoid slipping on the ice. What did the guy on the radio call this? Mixed precipitation? Easy for him to say from the comfort of his heated studio. Gobs of tiny snowflakes and little balls of ice continue their onslaught from above. Mixed precipitation is too friendly a term for this stuff.

The road curves, and I can make out the cabin up ahead. Not much farther now. The end is in sight. A hysterical kind of relief bubbles through me and is released in a giddy laugh that echoes above the tick, tick, tick of the pelting sleet.

Whoa! Another almost fall onto the hard ground.

I don't know which is best. If I keep my hands out to my sides to help steady myself, they're exposed to the cold and sleet. If I keep them balled in the pockets of my jacket, they're warmer, but I lose my balance. As I've demonstrated twice so far on this *hike*, it's easier to fall.

Could it really have been just this morning that I had coffee on my patio in a t-shirt and cotton pajama pants? Sure, I was in Texas, but the temperature was in the seventies. Never in my wildest dreams would I have imagined being here tonight in my hometown of Davidson, Virginia. Even when I saw the weather report at the airport, there was no mention of snow. It's barely November. We don't usually see this kind of storm around here until after Thanksgiving. So what if I didn't pack a real winter coat or boots, and so what if my rental car is stuck a ways back? At least I made it this far.

I will make it to the cabin. If the timing had been different, I might have missed my flight to Dulles altogether, and that would have sucked more than this. Brady needs me, and I'm not going to let him down.

One last push up the final rise.

Too fast.

My foot slips, and this time I don't catch myself. A scream escapes and then echoes through the wintry woods. Was that me? My butt hits the frozen ground with a thud. Pain shoots up my spine. I allow myself to lean back until I'm lying in the snow. I need to rest. Just for a few minutes.

Chapter Two

Hunter

Brady's not coming. He was supposed to be here by six. Now, it's going on eleven. My share of the pizza and chicken wings were polished off before eight, and then the storm started. I should have left at the first hint of sleet, but I didn't. It wasn't even supposed to storm. They called for possible snow flurries. Wrong again. The ground is now completely covered in a treacherous wintry mix. Brady drives an Audi coupe. Even his all-wheel drive isn't going to make it up this mountain tonight, and I'm not taking a chance going down, even in my Jeep.

I roll over and grab my cell phone from the nightstand. My fingers move to his name in my recent calls...again. *Come on, Brady. Answer your phone.* He doesn't. Again. Where the hell is he?

A big sigh propels me onto my side. I fluff my pillow and try to get comfortable. It's useless. Sleep isn't coming anytime soon.

A scream sounds in the night. A scream? Impossible. The nearest neighbor is almost a mile away from here, and why would he be out in this weather? Maybe a mountain lion? They shouldn't be out in this weather either.

What the hell?

Maybe it was a normal nighttime noise somehow magnified by the storm. Definitely reaching with this theory.

Shit. I have to check it out.

My legs slide to the side of the bed and then into my jeans in one quick motion. Brady's expecting me to be here. If it were him, then he would have yelled something by now. Plus, Brady would have been driving his car. No car engine to be heard. A look out the window doesn't show me anything other than the incredible view of snowfall by moonlight. Snow is like that. It's beautiful to watch from the inside, not so great most of the time that you're out in it.

I move quickly toward the family room, guiding myself down the short hallway by the tiny bits of moonlight that stream through the windows. Something makes me not want to turn a light on. My coat and boots are by the front door. I put them on as I stare out the front window again. Just to be on the safe side, I grab my Glock off the side table.

The wind carries the sound to me—weak and off-key, but most definitely, someone is singing.

"Just put one foot...you'll be walking out."

Shit. Now, I'm going to have to deal with some drunk person.

The snow and ice are slippery, but my boots help me quickly traverse the yard. She's easy enough to find, lying on her back near where the driveway joins the mountain road. She's not at all what I expected, and she's not drunk—she's freezing. Her eyes are closed. I haven't spoken yet, and she hasn't opened her eyes or acknowledged my presence. I quickly slip my Glock into my waistband and bend down next to her. It's hard to see too much out here, but I can see enough. She's not dressed for this weather: thin jacket, no hat or gloves, and not only is she not wearing boots, she's wearing shoes that don't even cover her feet. I take a deep breath and her scent fills my nostrils—lavender.

It can't be.

I lean in for a closer inspection. Long, wavy reddish-blond hair. Pert little nose, from above which, she's been looking down at me for years.

Kate Richardson.

Please, God, let her be okay. Please.

Kate Richardson has every right to be here. More right than I have since this cabin belongs to her family. But why in the world is she here? She belongs halfway across the country—literally. She lives in

Austin. How did she get here without a car? And most importantly, what is she going to do when she sees me?

Deep breath. Here we go.

"I'm going to lift you up now and carry you into the cabin. Can you hear me?"

Her eyes flicker open and study me. She's shivering so much that I'm not sure what she even sees. There's no more time to waste. I lean forward a little more, scoop her into my arms, and stand. She's not exactly light as a feather. She never was. She's more womanly than that with curves where women should have curves and real breasts.

Knock it off. Don't start thinking about those.

My walk back to the cabin is a lot slower as I carefully maneuver over the dark, frozen terrain. Now isn't the time to fall, but it isn't the time to dilly-dally either. I'd sure like to though. I breathe in her scent and hold it in my lungs. I've only been this close to Kate one other time, which was amazing and horrible at the same time. She can't realize it's me who's carrying her, or she would have had some kind of reaction.

I step up onto the porch and then move through the still-open front door and into the main room. The Richardson family cabin is fairly typical, I guess. There's one huge great room that takes up more than half of the square footage. Kitchen cabinets made from knotty pine, a sink, and a refrigerator line the far wall. A large island with four tall stools divides the kitchen from the dining area that holds a long farm table with ten chairs—a beautiful piece of polished maple made generations ago by a Richardson ancestor.

The dining area leads right to the family room. A large stone fireplace takes up this far wall. Two couches and a few upholstered chairs are arranged around the giant fireplace. It's a mix of furniture— castaways from the Richardson's homes in town— but it all comes together well enough.

I place her carefully in a sitting position on the biggest couch, hit the light, and brace myself for the scream. It doesn't come. *There should have been a scream.*

"Kate?"

No response. *This isn't good.*

She's in bad shape. *Please no frostbite.* Her cheeks are a ghostly white, not the flushed pink that usually comes from being out in cold weather. And it's no wonder. She sure isn't dressed for the freezing temperatures. Her jacket is way too thin, barely more than a fashion statement. My eyes move down her long legs to her feet. What the hell is she thinking with these shoes?

Then there's the fact that she hasn't reacted to seeing me here. She should be yelling at me. She should at least pull away. Her pale blue eyes stare back at me. They look responsive, but she isn't responding to anything that I'm doing. I kneel down in front of her and remove her flat leather shoes. It's all I can do to bite my tongue and not tell her how idiotic it was to go out in this weather wearing these things. Her feet are the same pale white as her cheeks, but there are no blisters or blueness to indicate severe frostbite. Good sign.

Next, I pull on the sleeve of her jacket. It's wet and needs to go. Her eyes widen—*finally a reaction*—but she still doesn't make a sound. It was probably the same reaction she'd have if she saw me walking down the street. She'd ignore me completely, but I won't let her do that this time.

"Your jacket is wet. You have to take it off."

No argument from Kate, but she relaxes her arms enough for me to remove it. The thin, blue sweater she wears isn't very wet, so that can stay on. I pull the afghan off the back of the couch and spread it carefully across her shoulders.

Her jeans need to come off, too, but I don't press my luck. I'm not an idiot. Instead, I leave her on the couch and busy myself with making a fire. It's warm in here, but it is not the kind of warmth she needs to stop her shivering.

Chapter Three

Kate

Hunter Simms. *Really?* Of all the people God could have put here in this cabin to help me. Why him?

He slips off his coat and boots. Sure, I'm shivering, and I must look like a complete mess from trudging up the mountain in the snow, but I'm not dead. As much as I can't stand him, even I have to admit that he's turned into quite the specimen of male perfection. Dark hair, chiseled face, and abs, too, apparently. I can't see them exactly, but I can tell that they're there through the fabric of his t-shirt. Those same gray-green eyes that have inserted themselves into my dreams and nightmares for too many years. And there's his butt that I have a full view of right there in front of me as he works to get the fire going. That butt that fits into those jeans like they were made just for him. *Wow*.

Sure, I was a bit out of it when Hunter spoke my name the first time in that husky voice of his that scrapes my insides. Too frozen and out of it to have much of an external reaction, but I was screaming on the inside. No one should be here. I'm supposed to be in and out of town without seeing anyone that I know. Well, anyone except for Brady. Seeing Hunter's worried eyes calmed me a little. Hunter hurt me all those years ago. At least he's here to help me now, and at this moment, I need all the help I can get.

With the fire now blazing, Hunter makes his way back to me. He carefully picks up each of my feet and studies them. They're tender to the touch but not necessarily painful. Then he examines my hands. Next, his gaze studies my face. I can't take it anymore. I have to make eye contact. My eyes move to meet his.

"What were you doing out there dressed like this?"

His voice is full of frustration, anger just below the surface. This is how we typically speak to each other—when we bother to speak to each other at all —words laced with contempt. I don't have the energy for this, but I have to defend myself.

Despite his angry tone, he takes my right hand gingerly between his own and lifts it to his mouth. His warm breath blows over my fingers in an effort to warm them.

"You aren't even wearing gloves."

He switches his efforts to my left hand now.

"I didn't exactly plan to be out in a snowstorm." *I'd say that's pretty obvious to both of us.*

"What are you doing here?"

"I could ask you the same question? This is my family's cabin. I have every right to be here. What about you?"

He sighs a huge sigh and plops down next to me on the couch.

"I was supposed to meet your brother. Brady asked me to meet him here tonight for dinner."

You have dinner with my brother?

"When was that?"

Hunter's brow furrows slightly. Guess that was an odd question to open with.

"Early this morning. He called around six-thirty."

"That's early for Brady. He doesn't usually get up before seven."

"I know. The whole thing was strange. He asked me to meet him here so he could give me something. I tried to get more out of him, but he said he would tell me everything tonight. I arrived here around six and let myself in." *Hunter knows where the key is kept?* "Brady hasn't shown. I don't expect him to at this point. He wouldn't make it up the mountain in this storm. Speaking of which, how did you?"

"I didn't, at least not all the way. My rental car slid off the road, and I had to walk the last part. Not sure how far but a ways."

"Well, why are you here? You're supposed to be in Texas."

How much do I tell him? Brady wanted Hunter to know about whatever's going on, but that was before he called me. He was extremely clear about what I have to do and that law enforcement *should not* be involved. Hunter's a policeman—definitely law enforcement. Something happened between six-thirty and nine o'clock this morning when he called me. Something important, I'm sure. But I have to give him some reason for being here.

"Brady called me this morning and asked me to come here." *That's true. Just not all the truth.*

"Why?"

"I don't know."

"Brady asked you to come here, so you dropped everything, jumped on a plane, and then drove up the mountain in an ice storm without asking why?"

"I did ask why." *I did.* "He just didn't tell me. He said that it was important, and I believed him." *That's mostly the truth.* I left out an important part, but I don't know *why* Brady wants me to do what he asked me to do. I just know that it's important. Brady is in some kind of trouble, and I'd do anything to help him.

Those gray eyes study me again, looking to see if I'm being truthful. Hunter's probably really good at assessing when someone is lying. That's part of his job as a police officer.

"But why you? Why would he ask *you* to travel all this way?"

Because I'm the only one who knows where it is. "I don't know. Maybe because I'm his sister, and he trusts me."

Make eye contact. Look confident. Don't give him reason to be suspicious.

Hunter's knuckles slowly graze my cheek. A tingle sparks at his touch and then turns into something more. The sensation ripples down my neck straight to the tightness in my belly. Is this part of the frostbite? Maybe the warming process? I lean away. He's touched me enough for one night. He smirks.

"If you don't like that, then you're not going to like my next suggestion. We need to get you out of those pants."

Without another word, Hunter stands and walks down the hallway. I concentrate on the flicking flames of the fire and try to get lost in the colorful embers. Is this some kind of cosmic joke? I'm stuck in a cabin with Hunter Simms. Why me?

Focus and stay strong. Don't let his tight abs, cute butt, and kind eyes get to you.

The memory floods back to me. It was the sixth grade. So long ago that I shouldn't still be hung up on it, and I'm not—hung up, that is. I just have a good memory, and twelve is a tough age. Old enough that you're trying to be older, but young enough that you don't know what you're doing. Maybe it's juvenile to care about something that happened sixteen years ago, but it was the first time that Hunter let me down.

It was the end of the school year, and I was nominated for the Student of the Year Award. It was a big deal—big enough that Mom took me out shopping for a new dress, and I got my first pedicure. My toes were flawless—they matched my petal pink dress perfectly—and they were peeking out of my also new white sandals. My first real heels, too. Like I said, it was a big day.

Hunter came over as we were lining up before parading into the gym. Gosh, I had such a crush on him—for years—since the second grade. I would look at him every chance I got, but I had barely said two words to him. I know I turned the color of my dress just because he was standing right in front of me. His dark brown hair was a bit disheveled, even though the rest of him was dressed up; he even wore a tie. It was green. Did his mom choose it because it matched his eyes? Then he spoke to me.

"Good luck, Katie."

I was so caught up in the moment that I didn't want to notice that he'd called me by the wrong name. Hunter Simms finally spoke to me, and he didn't know my name.

"It's Kate, actually. Not Katie."

His face flushed a little, and he smiled his shy, crooked smile. His eyes turned a little greener than their usual gray.

"I know your name. I just like Katie better. No one else calls you that."

"Oh."

My insides just turned to mush. I think I smiled. I was concentrating pretty hard on breathing at that point.

"Well, good luck today. With the award and all. You deserve to win."

"Thanks." I know that I wanted to think of more to say, but words wouldn't form. My brain was still processing his last words.

"Just wanted to let you know. Bye."

He was gone. Slowly, my brain began functioning again. Ideas of things I could have said to him came pouring in, taking my brain to overload. But, it was too late. Hunter had already moved to his place in line by Simon Simpkins. My eyes met those of Melanie, my still best friend, and we shared a telepathic scream of excitement that only best friends are capable of.

When my name was called as the Student of the Year winner, I didn't stand right away. I'd been listening intently for my name and was really hoping to hear it, but when it was announced, it took a few seconds for it to sink in. *I did it. I actually won.* My grades and extra-curriculars were all good enough —always the over-achiever—and my teachers loved me, but this award meant more because student votes counted, too.

I stood slowly and carefully made my way down

the big center aisle toward the stage. Everyone was applauding and cheering...for me. Mom's eyes found mine, and I saw the proud tears there. I made it up onto the stage without tripping on my new heels and felt an even bigger sense of accomplishment. Principal Ficarella was there, smiling down at me, already shaking my hand. The wooden plaque was a lot heavier than I thought it would be.

That's when I heard them. *"Geek! Geek! Geek!"* There weren't many people chanting, but enough that they could be heard over the applause. One look at Principal Ficarella told me that she could hear them, too. Embarrassment came in a wave of heat. Every part of my body became sweaty, including my feet, which slipped in my sandals as I ran off the stage. I tripped twice as I ran down the stairs, down the aisle between the chairs, and then out the door into the hallway. The tears started then, sprouting from my eyes. I didn't have a destination in mind but found myself in the music room. I didn't care where I was as long as I was alone.

Chapter Four

Hunter

"Do you think these will work?" Kate starts a little as if I just woke her from a dream. "They're too big, but they have a drawstring."

I hold the pants up in front of Kate so that she can see them. They're a bold red, yellow, and black plaid. Not something that she would probably ever wear in her new life where her shoes cost as much as a car payment. I don't know designer shoes, but I know that Brady complained about the cost of the pair that he bought her for her birthday last year. Now that Kate's so successful in Austin, she's changed.

Kate looks at the flannel pants distastefully—or

maybe that look was meant for me—and takes them.

"Can you manage changing by yourself?"

"Yes." The word comes out too quickly, but it gets her off the couch.

"I'll be in the kitchen. You should stay in front of the fire. I promise not to peek."

I flash her a smile in an attempt to lighten the mood and then get out of the way. The kitchen is only about ten feet from where she stands, but I stay true to my word and keep my back to her as I work. As much as I'd like to look, the reward isn't worth the risk. Kate's hated me for long enough that she wouldn't even be here alone with me if she didn't have to be. This is the most that we've said to each other in too many years to count. I don't want to push my luck.

It's funny how one decision—a decision made in a split second—can change your life. I have loved Kate from the first moment that I saw her in the second grade. It should have been obvious to everyone, since I barely spoke two words to her for more than four years. The day that I finally worked up the courage to talk to her was also the day that I made the decision that would mean she'd never want to talk to me again. No, that was more like the beginning of the end. There were a couple other times, but those didn't end well either.

Like that time in the eleventh grade when I gave Mark Barnet some *friendly advice* that he should stay away from Kate because she was a total bitch.

Kate heard about that and viewed it as another mark against me. I don't blame her. What she doesn't know is that I only told Mark that because he was bragging about how he was going to bang her and then ditch her. I had to do something to keep him away from her.

Maybe Kate has mellowed a bit over the years. She's already talked to me more tonight than she ever has.

It's clear that no one's been up here to the cabin for a while; there's nothing perishable in the kitchen. I could make coffee, but it's close to midnight. That's not going to work. Ahhh, but this will.

I start the water heating on the stove and dump the chocolate powder into two mugs.

"You okay in there?"

I sneak a little peek toward the fireplace. She's sitting on the couch again. *Good.* Looks like she was able to change her pants herself. As much as I'd liked to have helped with that task, it's much better that she could do it herself.

"I'm fine."

Not very convincing.

While Kate's feet didn't have any blisters, they are looking pretty rough. I fill the biggest pot I can find with warm tap water and carry it to her.

"You should soak your feet in warm water." She cringes. "It's not hot, just warm. It'll warm you up faster."

She moves her feet into the water, but I help with keeping the pajama pants from getting wet. Her shivering has subsided to nearly nothing, but it's still there and hampering her movements a bit.

Back to the kitchen now to whip up the hot chocolate. What did Brady say to Kate to get her to drop everything and get here this quickly? They are close, that's true, but it has to be more than that. Based on her reaction to seeing me here, she didn't even know that Brady and I are friends. I've grown pretty close to Brady and the rest of Kate's family over the last year. I've been wondering what she thought of that, but it's pretty clear now that they've been keeping the news from her.

Back to the fire.

Kate eyes me warily as I hand her the mug of hot cocoa.

"Oh, come on. I'm not going to poison you."

Realization flickers in her eyes. The corners of her mouth tip up to form a shy smile. Her head tilts just a little to the side as she looks up at me. It's been years since she's smiled at me. *Don't get carried away.* Two seconds ago, she looked at you like you were trying to kill her. Still, it's been years since she smiled at me that way. I'll take what I can get. I take it as a sign that it's safe to sit with her on the couch. I sit at the far end, leaving plenty of space between us, and take a sip of my own hot chocolate.

"Thanks for this. I can't remember the last time I had hot chocolate."

Another smile. *Nice.* Her cheeks are starting to get some color. Just a hint of pink, but a big improvement from the pale white of thirty minutes ago. The freckles that dot the bridge of her nose are more visible now. I've always loved those freckles.

"Well, I know when I last had hot chocolate." Her eyes meet mine over the rim of her cup. "Just last weekend. My sister and I went to a Virginia Tech football game. We were freezing, and I'd already had way too much coffee. She's hoping to go there next fall, so we went down for the day to check it out."

"I remember Kennedy. I just can't believe she's old enough to be going to college next year."

"She's older than that. Kennedy's already a sophomore. She's taking classes at the community college in Charlottesville before transferring to a university to finish her engineering degree."

Yet another smile. Maybe I did fall asleep waiting for Brady, and this is all a dream. There's no other explanation for how I'm sitting on a couch and sipping hot chocolate with Katie Richardson. Insane.

Chapter Five

Kate

"Is anything numb or really hurting as you warm up?"

My feet are burning. "No. I'm good."

"Right."

"When did you and Brady become so chummy? How did that happen?"

How could Brady not have told me? I fly halfway across the country to help him, and he's keeping secrets from me. Hunter eyes me warily.

"There was an attempted robbery at your family's store a little over a year ago."

"I remember. The guy pulled a gun on Mom while she was at the cash register, but Mom and Dad overpowered him and held him at gunpoint until the police arrived."

What the robber must have thought when Mom pulled out the shotgun and showed him what a real gun looks like. I feel myself smiling. How can I not? I wouldn't recommend that they do it again, but my parents are pretty darn awesome. No one has tried a serious robbery attempt in the hundred years that my family has owned that store, and now the world knows why. The Richardsons are tough.

"The chief was on another call at the time. I was the officer who arrived on the scene."

And that meant you had to be buddies with my brother?

"Your family knew who I was, but they were nice to me anyway. Brady and I got to talking about good places to fish, and one thing led to another, and he asked me if I wanted to come up here the next weekend." Geez. It sounds like they're secretly dating.

"And now you're best buds?"

Hunter shrugs his answer. *Thanks a lot, Brady. You traitor.* I fly across the country to help you and find out you've been chumming it up with—well, for as much as he knows—my arch enemy. No one except for my best friend, Melanie, knows I forgave Hunter years ago. Everyone else should still be under the impression that I hate his guts. How about some family loyalty? After I save Brady's butt, I'm going to kick it all the way back to Texas.

This conversation is over. I close my eyes and lean my head back to rest on the sofa.

More memories from that fateful day flood my brain. Melanie was the first to reach me. She didn't say anything at first. She just sat down next to me and put her arm around me while I cried. Mom and Dad found us after some amount of time, not sure how long we were there. My parents were irate. They were so loud. I wasn't ready for the anger stage yet. I was still so embarrassed, imagining what people must have thought of me.

"It was Hunter Simms. I heard him." Melanie spoke the words quietly, knowing how much they would hurt me.

And they did.

Why would Hunter take the time to congratulate me before the ceremony if he was just going to make fun of me later? Was that all part of his plan?

Principal Ficarella came in then with a couple teachers. Everyone was making such a fuss over me, and I hated it. It was too much to deal with. I stood up and did my best to dry my tears with the back of my hand. Dad put his arm around me and ushered me into the hallway to go home.

Of all people, Hunter Simms was standing outside the room waiting for us. He spoke my name, and my insides weakened. I didn't address him at all.

Instead, I turned away from Hunter and walked quickly down the hallway. He followed me, jogging to keep up.

"Kate, I'm really sorry. I didn't mean for that to happen."

He did sound sincere, and there was sorrow in his eyes, but I couldn't trust him.

"I didn't mean to say it in the first place, and I had no idea that they would start chanting. I don't think you're a geek, and you definitely deserve that award more than anyone else in the class."

Anger took over my whole being. Sure, I was still embarrassed, but the fury was there, too, pointing out the injustice of the situation. The last thing I wanted then was to hear his apologies. This was all his fault. He took the best day I'd ever had and turned it into the worst, most horrible day ever. I turned in his direction and threw my award at him. Apparently it wasn't a good throw because all he did was step out of the way. The plaque hit the wall, slamming into the sail of the Viking ship painted there, and then fell to the floor in several pieces.

My eyes open to find Hunter studying me. The fresh wave of anger that I felt from rehashing those same memories is tempered by the concern in his eyes. I need to get away from him to think, even if just for a minute. There's only one place where he won't follow me—the bathroom.

Chapter Six

Hunter

Kate is doing really well considering the condition that I found her in outside. If anything ever happened to her...but, it didn't. I was here to help her, and she's okay. She just walked to the bathroom by herself. She'll be fine. Of course I'm glad that I was here to help her, but there's another part of me that knows the hurt that will come of it. No one has the ability to rock my world like Kate does. Seeing her again brings everything back, and no matter how long it's been, some of the feelings are raw.

That must be how it is for Kate, too. She's always been so angry about what happened back in the sixth grade. It only got worse later when I stood her up in the tenth grade. Those memories are always what she goes back to when she thinks of me. I get it. I fucked up. But it was a long time ago. I think about that often enough, but the part of our history that haunts me is much more recent—the summer after high school graduation.

It was the weekend before many of us were leaving for college. Simon Simpkins had the going away party of the century, or at least it seemed that way. Simon's house was huge, which was good because pretty much our entire graduating class was there, even me, and I never went to parties. At that point in my life, I had way more important things to do. But, Simon practically begged me, so I went.

My friends were pounding the drinks, trying to get wasted in as short an amount of time as possible. Three beers in, and I wondered what I was doing there. Was this worth taking a night off from work? I wandered through the rooms trying to decide. Simon's house was a total mess. Discarded plastic cups and other trash littered the floor. People were everywhere—some drinking and talking, others in various stages of making out. My head was starting to spin. I went down to the basement thinking it might be quieter.

It wasn't. If anything, there was more energy down here. Music was playing, and Marlene Jeffries stood at the bottom of the basement stairs holding a large plastic bowl. Entrance to the basement required that your name went into the bowl. I complied without even knowing what it was for.

Well, I found out soon enough. *Seven minutes in heaven.* Sure, I'd heard of it, and apparently, I was about to take part in the game, because my name was the first one selected from the bowl. *Did they even stir it up?* I tried to decline, but Marlene wouldn't have it. I gave up fighting it and waited to see which girl I would be with for my time in *heaven.* Kate Richardson's name was called. *No flippin' way.* I remember wondering if Marlene called her name on purpose, just to mess with us. Everyone knew that Kate hated me.

I turned in a circle looking for her. She was there, completely red-faced, being pushed toward me by the crowd. She was trying to protest, too, but it was useless. Hands were pulling and pushing me, and they didn't stop until we were both in the closet. Kate grabbed for the doorknob just as the lock clicked from the outside. We were smushed together between the out-of-season clothing. That was the point of the game. Her lavender scent filled the space. *Maybe this is what heaven smells like*, I thought. It would have been more heavenly if Kate actually wanted to be there with me.

She tried to lean back, and she did a little, enough so that her chest wasn't flush with mine. But, that little movement pressed the lower half of her body closer, and my body sprung to life. She froze in that position, likely deciding that moving around would only make it worse for her.

I could feel the heat emanating from her body. She was furious, but there was nothing that we could do. Kate was stuck with me for seven minutes. I was going to make the most of it. I thought I'd open with a compliment.

"You gave a great valedictorian speech at graduation."

"Whatever. Like you care what a geek has to say."

Her comeback didn't surprise me. She'd managed to ignore me off and on since that fateful day in elementary school. I was used to it.

"I apologized. I never meant for that to happen. I didn't even think you were a geek. I still don't."

It felt even hotter at that moment.

"Then why did you say it? It was so mean."

"It wasn't like that. The truth is that I really liked you, and Simon figured it out—not cool in the sixth grade. He saw me talking to you when we were lined up in the hallway before graduation. His teasing was relentless. I called you a geek to throw them off. It was stupid, but I was a sixth-grade boy who just wanted it to stop. I was embarrassed. How could I know they would start chanting? I tried to get them to stop. I swear."

"You're full of crap and drunk."

"I have had a couple beers, but I'm not drunk. This is the first time that you've talked to me since the first

part of sophomore year, and I have a good excuse for letting you down then, too. You have to hear me out because you're locked in here with me."

"It was a long time ago, but it was horrible. People still call me geek. Did you know that?"

"Yeah, and I'm sorry for that. I've paid for it, too."

"It couldn't have bothered you too much. You beg me for a chance to make it up to me until I finally give in and agree to one date. Then you stand me up."

"I wanted to be there. More than anything."

"You didn't even explain it to me. You just wrote me a note."

"Would you have listened to me? You've hated me ever since."

Kate sighed a huge sigh. Her breath tickled my ear, causing my body to respond by creating even less space between us. She had to notice. She showed no reaction that I could see, but it was super dark in that tight space.

"I don't hate you."

Just like that, the slightest glimmer of hope spawned in my chest.

"You don't?"

"No, not anymore. And since we seem to be getting things off our chests, I want to tell you that I'm really sorry about your mom." My breath left me like I'd been punched in the gut. Her words hit me that hard. "I really wanted to tell you that when your mom passed away, but I didn't know how. I'm sorry, Hunter."

I didn't mean to kiss her then. I didn't plan it. My lips moved to hers totally on their own. At first, they were still, just relishing the fact that they were connected to Kate's. Then it happened. I moved just the slightest amount, and the world shifted. You could say that there were fireworks, but it was more like the entire house exploded.

My arms moved around her, pulling her to me. There was zero space between us. Her fingers moved through my hair, and her tongue found mine. *Her tongue*. Total shock and awe. *It really was heaven*.

And then it was over. The door wrenched open. Kate pulled away. Her eyes locked with mine for the briefest second. To this day, I still have no idea what emotion was in them. She turned, ran up the stairs, and was gone. I ran after her, barely registering the catcalls of the people around me.

She was gone.

That was the last time I saw Kate until I found her in the snow.

Ten years.

It's been ten years since that night, and that's an awful long time to wonder what her look meant. Was all of that an effort to get back at me for what I did to her years before? Could Kate really be that manipulative? Did she want me to follow her? If she did, she sure didn't try to be caught. I looked all over for her that night, and I went to her house the next day. Her mother said that she wasn't home, but her car was in the driveway. Kate left for the University of Texas a few days later and then never came home. Sure, she came back for holidays and a vacation here and there, but she never came back to live. I've heard bits and pieces about her through the years and more lately since I've been friendlier with her family. She's successful now. All fashionable and whatnot.

It's not like I had time to pine over her. I didn't go away to school, but I always had a job to do, and sometimes more than one. I pushed Kate Richardson far to the back of my brain and tried to get on with living my life. Seeing her again has thrown me, but I will have to guard myself against any long-term effects.

Chapter Seven

Kate

Relief. A bathroom visit helped. I really needed to get away from Hunter. Just being near him again makes me...I don't know what, but it's uncomfortable. He makes all these feelings churn up inside me, and I don't want them to. I like them put away nicely wherever they go when I'm not with him.

The lights flicker and then darkness.

Great. The power's out.

"Kate? Are you okay?"

"Yeah. I'm fine."

Better get back out there, or he'll come looking for me.

Sure enough. Hunter stands in the hallway right

outside the bathroom door.

"I'm okay."

He doesn't pick me up or even touch my elbow to guide me. He just walks with me back to the couch. The family room is still well lit, thanks to the fire. It's also warm in here, which will be a very nice thing now that there's no heat. I sit down in the same spot on the couch. Hunter grabs another blanket and sits next to me, closer this time.

The Hunter with me now is just a grown-up version of the boy who spoke to me in that hallway that day. He's filled out very nicely. His hair is a little darker now, and his eyes are, too. He's aged well despite the little lines that crinkle at the edges of his eyes and mouth when he smiles. They somehow make him more attractive. *Down girl.* Talk about something.

"Do you like being a policeman?"

"Sure. It's a good job. It pays well, and I get to help people. That's mostly what it is. There's not a lot of crime in Foster County. What do you do? Something with decorating, right?"

Guess he would know that since he's so chummy with my family.

"Sort of. I have a blog, and I write for a couple magazines."

"You make a living doing *that*?" Hunter's eyebrows rise in disbelief. *Jerk.*

"Yes, actually."

"So, people pay you to decorate their homes?"

"No. I come up with decorating ideas and post them on my blog. I get paid from the advertising, and I get paid when I sell articles to home magazines. I've even had a couple television spots. They were just local shows, but it was still TV."

"People are too wasteful with their money."

"What the hell does that mean?"

"It means just what I said. People who have money don't understand what it's like for those of us who don't have it. It's theirs to waste if they want to, but I think that's what it is. A waste."

His eyes are hard. He speaks through his thin mouth. What happened? Hunter was so nice earlier. He made me hot cocoa. How does talk of decorating get him so ticked off? Hunter degrading my whole profession isn't exactly making me happy.

"First of all, people who have money can spend it on whatever they want to. And secondly, my whole thing is that I help people design on a budget. I give them ideas for projects where they can use things that they might already have around the house. Things that don't require a lot of money."

Why am I suddenly having to defend myself to Hunter Simms?

Why does he care how much people spend on decorating?

"I'm just saying that decorating a house isn't a necessity."

"You're talking about my career." No response from Hunter. He just stares at me with those freakin' eyes of his. "Do you have a problem? Why were you nice to me before? You're suddenly being hostile."

"Why aren't you telling me why you're really here?" His nostrils flare.

"Why are you doing this? Are you trying to start an argument?"

Chapter Eight

Hunter

What the hell am I doing?

Maybe I am trying to find reasons to fight with Kate. Just being near her is too much for me. She's infiltrated my good sense, and I can't let her do that. I can't let her get under my skin. She drives me so fucking crazy.

Kate stares back at me with those beautiful blue eyes of hers, made even more alluring by the fire. I don't know whether to yell at her or kiss her. Kiss her. Nothing would be better. I know what she feels like. I know what she tastes like. Her lips are just right there, parted, as if waiting for me to take them.

"Are you going to kiss me?"

My brain takes a few seconds to register her question. Not just the words, but her meaning. Did she speak in a breathy whisper as if begging me to kiss her or were her words spoken in disbelief, like how could I even think of such a thing? Definitely the latter. I was just trying to pick a fight with her. Why was I trying to fight with her?

"I promise. I wasn't going to kiss you." *Not yet, anyway. I was just thinking about it.* My brain finally kicks in. "Kissing is off limits."

"Off limits?" Kate's eyes are wide with disbelief. "Why? Do you have a girlfriend? Are you married?"

"No. There's no girlfriend, and I'm sure you would have heard if I was married." Her relief is visible, although I'm not sure why.

"What about you? Any special cowboys down there in Texas?"

"No."

"I thought I heard there was."

"Not anymore." That subject is clearly off limits.

The heat of her gaze warms my face.

What does she want from me? This is Kate Richardson. If she wants to kiss me, it would only be because of the situation—snowstorm, no power, warm fire. Kate said it herself, she's only staying in Davidson for the weekend, and then she's heading back to her life in Texas. I'm not doing this to myself again, no matter how much I'm pulled to her.

"We should both get some sleep."

I stand and poke at the fire. It's more like I'm

stabbing the fire, but it can take it. I add another log and stab at it some more.

"Are you warm enough?"

She nods, her expression unreadable.

"Goodnight, Kate."

I snatch my blanket and lie down on the other couch, cold and alone. But, over here, I won't have to worry about breaking my promise.

Chapter Nine

Kate

It was a long, cold night, and it didn't have to be. Not temperature cold. The blazing fire kept me plenty warm enough—I'm pretty sure Hunter stoked it a few times during the night. I mean emotionally. How do we do that to each other? We drive each other crazy. It's obvious that, for whatever reason, Hunter was trying to pick a fight with me. He was so considerate in so many ways. He saved me, plain and simple. Then, he started picking a fight, and before he was finished griping at me, he looked like he was going to kiss me.

I should have kept my mouth shut so he would have gone through with it.

Plus, what about the whole *we need to huddle together for warmth* thing? What kind of guy doesn't pull that line? I thought I was the one who hated Hunter, not the other way around. He seemed to like me well enough when we were in that closet together. He was drunk then, so maybe that's the difference. The time in that closet meant more to me than it did to Hunter. I've always known that. However, the events of last night just don't add up.

The fire is still going strong. I stretch and take stock of my body. I can wiggle my toes and my fingers. They don't hurt much, just a little sore. Excellent. There's no time to waste in dealing with frostbite. I need to find what I came for and then figure out a way off this mountain. My meeting is at one o'clock. The big unknown is travel down the ice-covered road. Will I be able to get my rental car unstuck? Will I have to ask Hunter to drive me? No idea how I would pull that off. Hunter would never go for it, and I can't tell him what I'm up to. I will walk there if I have to. Brady is counting on me. The way he sounded on the phone...he's in huge trouble. His life could even be in danger.

What has he gotten himself into?
What have I gotten myself into?

Whatever it is, I need to get it taken care of and get out of town before I run into my parents. They'll be worried if they find out Brady asked me to come here. But something tells me they'll be even more upset to find out about whatever Brady is involved in. I'll see them next week for Thanksgiving and then again at Christmas.

Is that coffee? The scent wafts through the room. That's incentive enough to get out of bed. There's also the bathroom; I really need to go. I stand gingerly on my feet and pad quietly down the short hallway to the bathroom.

The reflection that looks back at me is not impressive. My color looks good, which means I can get past that and now focus on the mascara that's caked under my eyes. I do my best to wash it off with the bar soap from the shower, trying not to get it in my eyes. Now, the black marks are gone, but my eyelids are totally puffy, and the whites of my eyes are decidedly pink. Oh, so attractive.

With a big sigh, I head for the kitchen. Coffee awaits and so does Hunter. *Just get it over with.*

Hunter leans against the wall, a cup of coffee in his hand, staring out the window. He doesn't turn around. I'm not exactly stealthy. He has to hear me. *What does that mean?* This is not going to continue.

"Hunter?"

I lightly touch his shoulder. He turns to face me, and I see a new Hunter. Dark whiskers line his cheeks and chin. To say *he needs a shave* wouldn't do him justice. A shave is the last thing he needs. This is definitely a good look for him. His eyes are light green today, intense and searching, although for what, I don't know. He wears the same t-shirt and butt-hugging blue jeans.

"Good morning."

Those two simple words in that deep voice of his scrape at the armor that protects me from Hunter. Do I still need protecting from him?

"Look," I drop my arm to my side. "I know things got a little heated between us last night, but I don't want us to fight with each other anymore. Can we try again?"

Hunter smiles a very large, very crooked, totally mouth-watering smile.

"I can't believe it. Kate Richardson wants to be friends."

A smile forms on my lips, too.

"I do, Hunter. Thank you for saving me last night."

"It's a good thing you were singing. I might not have found you out there otherwise."

My eyes widen to the size of flying saucers.

"I was singing?"

Hunter nods with a chuckle, and then his smile falls flat.

"I don't know what I would have done if you had frozen to death just outside of the house. If you hadn't screamed, then I never would have known you were there."

His eyes are gray now. They changed color right in front of my eyes. So, they're green when he's smiling and gray when he's serious. There are many other emotions to catalogue.

"You were almost to the cabin. Why were you just lying there?"

"I don't know." *I really don't.* "I fell down. I remember that. Then I just remember feeling tired. I didn't plan on staying there for long. I was just taking a break." Now Hunter's eyes widen. "It seemed like a good idea at the time."

My lips brush his cheek. I'd say they did it on their own, but I don't think that's actually possible. Hunter leans back and eyes me suspiciously.

"Why did you just kiss me?"

"I don't know."

"No kissing."

"Hunter, it was a kiss on the cheek. A thank you for saving me."

"Not a good idea."

What the heck? Is this a religious thing? Is Hunter saving himself for his future wife? He sure didn't seem to be saving himself when we were in that closet together.

Dumbfounded, I pour myself a cup of coffee and find the sugar bowl. Wait. The pot is working. *The electricity is back on.*

When there's nothing left to talk about, talk about the weather.

"How does it look out there?"

I stand at the other side of the window across from Hunter and stare outside. The sun shines brightly even though it's not yet very high in the sky.

"It's forecasted to be warm and sunny today. All of this should melt soon enough. Let's give it a couple hours before we try to get your car out."

"Okay." *Good. I don't feel like walking all the way to Candle Run.* "Were you able to get in touch with Brady this morning?" I know that Hunter hasn't talked with Brady, but I have to keep up the pretense that I don't know where Brady is. Unfortunately, that's very true. I have no idea where he is.

He shakes his head. "I called him a few minutes ago, but it just went to voicemail. I'm not sure what that means."

It means that I think he's tied up. I just hope not literally. A jolt of panic shoots through me. *Act normal.* Don't freak out in front of Hunter. He'll ask too many questions.

"I hope hanging around here with me, waiting for the snow to melt, doesn't impact your day too much. Did you have any special Saturday plans?"

Hunter sets his coffee mug down on the table and then folds his arms in front of him. He stares back at me with medium gray eyes. Gray is conversational?

"No. Normally with an ice storm, I'd go into work, but the chief says things are under control. Looks like most people were smart and hunkered down where they were for the night instead of trying to drive in it. Being that it's the weekend, not as many people are trying to get to work."

Speaking of getting to work.

"I'm going to go out for a hike."

"A hike? Now?"

"Yeah. That's what I usually do when I come up

here. Just a quick one. I won't be gone for long."

"Didn't you get enough of a hike last night?"

I chuckle. Hopefully the gesture doesn't come off as faked. Hunter's just staring at me.

"This time I'll borrow Mom's boots and jacket. That'll help."

"Knock yourself out."

The temperature outside isn't warm, but the sun sure is. The heat of it warms my back as I walk, and it's turning the ice of last night into slush, making traversing the mountain one hundred times easier. I'm not going far anyway—only about a hundred yards from the back door of the cabin. I left from the front though and meandered around a little before heading in this direction. Hunter's curious, and he needs to stay out of whatever this is.

The sights and smells of this place bring back an onslaught of memories. We practically lived up here during the summers when we were kids. I took my first steps in the front yard. Brady and I both learned how to ride a two-wheeler here. There were too many cuts and scrapes to count, all from exploring every inch of these woods.

Our fort is right where it always was and easy for me to find, even with this dusting of snow. It's been years since Brady and I spent our days tromping through these woods, but some things you just don't forget. I have to bend to get through the door, but the structure looks mostly the same, just a lot smaller. The purple paint on the inside has faded, but it still works to brighten the place up. I spent my own allowance on that can of paint and thirty minutes at the hardware store staring at swatches to pick out just the right shade. I was nine years old. I'm pretty sure that was the beginning of my design career.

Dad and Gramps built this one room fort for us that summer. We had tried to piece something together ourselves, but when Brady broke his leg during our construction process, Mom made Dad get involved. Then Gramps wanted to lend a hand, and it became a real project.

The fort is rectangular in shape and measures five feet by twelve feet—I still remember. The open entrance is on one side and there are windows cut on each of the other three sides. There's a small wooden table and two chairs on one end and a wooden treasure chest on the other. All are a little worse for wear now, but they're still here.

It's fitting that Brady hid this mystery bag in our treasure chest. I lift the lid carefully, unsure of what I'll find. *Please no snakes.* As brave as I was about running through these woods, I was never brave when it came to snakes. Big relief when the chest is empty of woodland creatures. It contains only a few rocks that we probably put there as children, and what I came for.

I lift the bag out and stare at it in wonder.

It's a cosmetic bag.

I lean towards the window so that I have more light.

It's pink with yellow and purple flowers—pretty hideous actually. Why would Brady want this? I unzip the bag and see various cosmetics staring back at me. Is this really what he wants? One more check of the wooden box, and it's pretty clear that it has to be this bag, but it makes no sense.

Whatever you do, don't involve the police.

It's make-up. I don't get it.

Brady, you better have a good explanation for this.

Chapter Ten

Hunter

So that's why Kate's here. She needed to retrieve whatever that is she now has in her hands. Can't quite make it out from this distance, even with binoculars. Whatever it is, it's important enough that she risked driving here in an ice storm to get it. Does whatever it is have to do with Brady's mysterious disappearance? Is he in danger? Kate's being truthful when she says that Brady asked her to come here, but there are things that she's hiding. She's a horrible liar. She's stubborn enough, though, that I can't push her on it, or she'll just dig in her heels, and I'll never learn the truth.

Kennedy calls and confirms that everything's

okay at home. Granny's okay, too. They were already home for the night when the sleet started. Although I wasn't all that worried about them, I still appreciate that Kennedy made the effort to call me. If she doesn't want me to be overprotective, then she has to be smart and tell me things.

The fire's died down enough now that it'll be okay to leave. I set the screen in front of the opening and do some other tidying up. There isn't much to do; just fold the blankets and make the bed that I used to toss and turn around in before Kate arrived. It was like my brain couldn't turn off. Like maybe it knew that something big was about to happen.

Who would have guessed that Kate would be back in my life again? No matter how much I try not to be happy that she's here, I can't stop thinking about her. The skin on my cheek still burns where she kissed me this morning. She's going to leave again, and it's going to be painful.

Kate walks inside wearing a guilty smile. Geez, she's really bad at this. I'd know she was up to something even if I hadn't watched her while she was on her *hike*. She's holding her arm awkwardly, bracing it against her side to support whatever it is that she has hidden inside her jacket.

Pretend like there's nothing to see.

"Have a good walk?"

Her smile widens, too forced to be real.

"It was great. Just like I remember it."

"Uh huh." *Let it go. Do not ask her about whatever*

mission she was on out there in the woods. "There's cold pizza for breakfast. I know you're used to fancier food and all, but that's all I've found that's worth eating."

"That would be great. I love cold pizza for breakfast."

Yeah. Right. Her last boyfriend took her to Paris where she ate crepes at a sidewalk cafe for breakfast each morning. I saw photos at her parents' house.

We walk to the kitchen area, and I hand her the take-out box. She doesn't remove her coat or even unzip it. She takes the box from me using her free hand, sets it on the island, opens it, and works awkwardly to get a slice free from the others with just one hand. Her eyes dart up to mine. *Don't say anything.* Instead, I fill two glasses with water and join her for breakfast.

"I owe you an apology. I'm sorry that I made fun of your work." Her eyes soften as she stares at me over her pizza slice. "I'm sure you do a great job."

"But you don't think it's necessary."

"It's not something that I care about, but I know that it's important to others, so I'm sure you make them happy." *Much better. Please don't be mad at that.*

"Why not you? Don't you care about where you live? Don't you want it to be a nice place?"

"It doesn't have to be." She's not buying that. A very large sigh escapes. "Home for me just needs to be somewhere that's safe. With plenty to eat. That's enough."

That went too far. Kate's eyes aren't angry—no, it's much worse than that. They're filled with pity. *Shit. I did not want to go there.*

"I'm sorry that I'm so dense. I should have known what you were trying to tell me."

I shrug. What the hell, we've come this far with this conversation.

"Money was hard to come by for my family after mom passed away. It was difficult to put food on the table and pay for absolute necessities. I learned early on not to spend money on things that aren't important. If other people have money for frivolous things, then more power to them."

"I told you. My whole point is that you can make your home nice on the cheap. You don't have to spend a lot of money."

"Yeah, but when you're working as much as you possibly can, there's no time or energy to put toward making things pretty. There's enough to do with the maintenance and upkeep of a place."

Kate's watching me as I try to explain myself. She still doesn't look angry, and the pity seems to be gone for the most part, but who knows what's going on in there?

"Look, I'm not trying to play the "*Oh woe is me!*" card, I'm not saying that your work has no value, and I'm not trying to piss you off. I'm just trying to be honest with you."

Kate adjusts whatever is under her coat and then

presses her waist against the island to let the countertop support it. *This is killing me.* Should I bust her with whatever this is and make her tell me what she's up to? *What is she keeping from me?*

"What about when you were young and your mom was alive? Did she work to make your home beautiful?"

Didn't expect that.

"Mom made things nice in her own way. She didn't decorate based on ideas from books, but she made sure that our house was a home."

"That's what it's all about. I'll be the first to admit it. I just want to help people get that warm, comfy feeling in their homes. What are some of the things that your mom did? I bet she proudly displayed your school pictures on the wall?"

Memories of what home used to be like come in a rush. After-school snacks, loving hugs, and parents who cared about report cards. I close my eyes to remember more and to hide the feelings that go with them. There's no point in dwelling on the past, and it's not something I allow myself to do. How does Kate make my emotions zing all over the spectrum? It's not good to *feel* so much.

My eyes open again to study Kate. She's thoughtful, but she doesn't look like she's expecting an answer, which is good because I'm not talking about this anymore. She reaches across the island and places her hand on my forearm. Her warmth makes my skin sizzle beneath my cotton shirt.

Why is she touching me? Don't get me wrong, I think I like it. No, I *know* I like it, but I have to protect myself. Things with Kate invariably end in disaster.

"When are you going back home?"

She starts, sucking in a small breath and raising her hand. She crinkles her nose as her hand hovers above my arm. She pulls it back toward her, folds her hands together, and leans her elbows on the countertop in front of her. Her eyes meet mine, but she can't seem to keep the contact as she alternates between looking at me and looking at her folded hands.

"My flight leaves tomorrow afternoon."

Yep. Disaster. My own head shakes. Kate lives in Texas. It only makes sense that she'll go back home. This cabin suddenly feels way too small. The sooner I put some distance between us, the better.

Chapter Eleven

Kate

Those eyes. They're killing me.

There's a lot going on in there right now, and I have no clue what it is. I should have understood about Hunter's family situation. Wish I would have caught on before he had to explain it to me. This is a small town—not a lot of secrets to be had. It's a well-known fact that Hunter's home life fell apart after his mother passed away. His father started using drugs, and Hunter worked to feed his younger brother and sister. Not long after we graduated high school, their father left them completely, and everything fell on Hunter.

I've always respected him for that, the way he stepped up and took on all that responsibility. I forgave him for what he did to me a long time before his father left. It was when his mom was sick. She became ill in the fall of our sophomore year and was sick for months with liver cancer. Hunter still came to school most days, but it took a huge toll on him. His eyes looked more and more haunted with each passing day. My eyes softened toward him first, and soon all of me did. No one should have to feel that much sorrow. His hurt was life or death, and although mine seemed major at the time, it was superficial compared to what Hunter had gone through.

Mom had about had it with me after Hunter's mother passed away. She wanted me to do the compassionate thing and express my condolences to him personally. I wanted to talk to him, but at the same time, I had no idea what to say. I couldn't let anyone know that my feelings had changed. I don't know why not, but everything about Hunter felt so intensely personal.

One afternoon after school, I got the courage to visit him. I told Mom that I was going to Melanie's. Again, I don't know why I couldn't tell her the truth. It's what she wanted me to do, but the words didn't come. My belly was a ball of nerves as I pulled up to

Hunter's house. There was no car in the driveway, but I'd come this far, so I charged up the porch steps and knocked on the door.

Mr. Simms answered. He didn't say any words of greeting. He just stared at me for a moment. The scent of stale beer permeated the air along with the sadness of his loss. He looked every bit the grieving widower with his droopy eyes and wrinkled clothes.

I swallowed the lump in my throat and asked for Hunter. The sadness in his eyes swirled into an angry stare. *He's not here. Get the hell off my porch.* I did. I ran back to my car and got out of there as fast as I could. I pulled over about a mile down the road and let the tears come.

Poor Hunter. What it must have been like to live in that house. He would have been so embarrassed if he knew that I'd seen his father that way. So, I told no one—not Melanie and not my mom—even when she grounded me for a week because I wouldn't pay condolences to Hunter and his family after their loss. She was furious that I would hold a grudge for so long against him. Still, I should have found a way to tell Hunter sooner instead of waiting until we were forced into a closet together years later. He was drunk then and probably doesn't remember that night. Does he even remember that I forgave him? Does he remember our kiss? The heat of a burning blush travels up my neck. That kiss scared the crap out of me. There's never been another one like it.

Don't go there now. Think about it later when Hunter isn't watching. *There's a job to do.*

"Do you think the roads are safe now? We should probably get going."

"Yeah. Probably."

Hunter turns off the lights and lowers the thermostat while I pack the few things I have into a plastic grocery sack. This works well because it gives me a place other than my coat to hide the mystery make-up bag. The stupid thing is too big to fit in a pocket. Hunter's given me more than one curious look. I'm just glad that he hasn't actually questioned me about it.

Hunter locks the front door and replaces the key on its little shelf under the porch. He knows where the key is kept. *Crazy.* It still amazes me that he and Brady are friends. And for more than a year. When was Brady going to tell me?

Hunter and I both hop into his Jeep.

"Cool truck. I love the color."

I really do. It's a deep mossy green. What would Hunter be feeling if his eyes were this color?

He mumbles a thank you and drives away from the cabin.

"You walked a long way last night. We're lucky

that you just got a bit of frostnip. Frostbite would have been a whole lot worse."

Tell me about it. That would have been way too much to deal with right now. My rental is there on the side of the road where I abandoned it, about half a mile from the cabin. The snow and ice around the tires haven't melted away, but it is softer, more of a slush, really. The car starts on the first try and with a little push from Hunter, is released from its snowy entrapment. I put it in park, leave it running, and then climb out to talk with Hunter.

He stands about two feet away from me, his hands in the pockets of his jacket. His eyes are a stark gray color that goes really well with his unshaven cheeks and chin. He feels so far away. The idea of saying goodbye to him weighs heavily on my chest. Where did this come from? If Brady didn't need my help, would I say goodbye? It doesn't matter, because if it weren't for Brady's current predicament, I wouldn't be here with Hunter in the first place.

I chance a step closer. He retreats by the same distance. First, he won't kiss me, and now he won't even stand near me. Why?

"Thank you again for saving me last night. I could have died out there if it weren't for you."

"I guess it's fortunate for both of us that you belt out tunes when you're in danger. You could use some voice lessons though, no offense."

He made a joke. We share a little chuckle, and I

punch him in the arm for good measure. *Geez.* It's like we're in grade school all over again.

"Would you like to have dinner with me tonight?"

The words are out before my brain registers that they were spoken. I wait in breathless anticipation while Hunter chews over my offer. We'd have to go somewhere in Charlottesville where we won't risk running into anyone that I know since my parents aren't supposed to know that I'm here.

Hunter looks down at the ground and shuffles his feet before answering. Feels like an eternity.

"I can't tonight. I already have plans."

"Well, I'll be back in town soon for Thanksgiving. Maybe I can see you then?"

Why did I ask that? He said no. *Where is my dignity?*

"Sure."

He said yes.

All these feelings pump their way through me, leaving me unsure of how I feel about anything. Hunter has hurt me before. Am I a fool for trying again? I'm hopeful that I will get to see him when I come back for Thanksgiving, and to top it all off, I'm frightened about why I feel any of this. Does Hunter feel it, too?

Why won't he kiss me?

Hunter's hands come out of his pockets, but he folds them in front of his chest. His protective stance couldn't be any more obvious. I forgave him. Are we ever going to get over this weirdness between us?

"Kate, you know that I'd do anything to help you, right. Just tell me, and I will help."

He knows.

Hunter is law enforcement. The instructions were clear.

"I know."

I can't take it anymore. I close the distance between us before Hunter has a chance to move away. His folded arms are an impediment, but they won't stop me. I weave my own through his and hug him until he's forced to put his arms around me as well.

And he does.

His arms hold me tightly against his hard chest, and I feel wrapped in the promise of safety and security. *Everything is going to be okay.* I breathe in his manly scent of aftershave, pine needles, and fire. This is what it's supposed to feel like when you're held by a man. This is what I've never felt with anyone else, even Clint. Just like there's never been a kiss that compares with Hunter's all those years ago.

His arms stiffen, and just like that, the magic is over. He steps back like he just received a shock, like he's afraid to touch me.

What the hell?

Hunter's eyes make their transition from green to gray. What changed? Does he not feel the same way I do? Maybe we're just never going to be okay. Tears are close. Hunter can't see those, and besides, I don't have time for any of this. Brady needs me.

"Goodbye, Hunter."

With a big sigh, I get in my car and drive away. He doesn't stop me or say another word, not even goodbye.

Why does he always have to be so difficult?

I wipe my teary eyes again with the back of my hand.

What did I do in a previous life to deserve this? Hunter Simms was put on this earth to make me miserable. What are the chances that he and I would be snowed in together in a cabin? *Buy a lottery ticket; it's your lucky day.* Or not. It's more likely that I'd be struck by lightning. At least dealing with Hunter has kept my mind off of Brady's mess. Now, I get to stress about both.

The meeting is scheduled for one o'clock at Pigeon Park Bridge. Pigeon Park is an out-of-the-way wooded area about five miles outside of town. The story goes that a local farmer proposed to his sweetheart next to the little stream that runs through the property. They were married for more than fifty years, and after she passed away, he donated the land to the town so that everyone could enjoy the beautiful spot. The story doesn't explain why he named it Pigeon Park. Maybe he called her Pigeon. This is a quiet spot in the summer. In the winter, it's desolate—the perfect location for some kind of clandestine meeting.

I pull my rental into the small parking lot; it only holds about four cars at the most.

It's twelve-thirty. I'm early.

Like thirty minutes early.

Too much time to sit and wait and wonder.

With a heavy sigh, I open the make-up bag to take a closer look. It's still just make-up, and it even looks used. What's life or death about some nasty old make-up? I remove the contents piece by piece. It's the usual stuff: blush, a brown eyeshadow set, mascara, a few make-up brushes, concealer, foundation, and powder.

Look harder. Something has to be here. This stuff is somehow worth Brady's life.

The loose powder container is the biggest item, but it doesn't look out of the ordinary. I twist off the round lid, holding my breath. A powder puff. Not exactly shocking. Lifting that reveals a plastic separator. I pry that out, and, as expected, find loose powder.

But wait a minute. Something else is in here. Something solid pokes through the top of the powder. I pinch the small object and rub it between my fingers to remove the powder.

It's—*oh no, Brady*—a diamond.

What have you gotten yourself into?

A quick search of the little round container reveals that it's practically full of diamonds. I quickly replace the little separator and puff and place all the make-up back into the bag.

There's powder on me. They'll know I looked.

I brush it off Mom's jacket and my pants and then check my face in the mirror.

Why did I look in the bag? Just because I was searching for something to get my mind off of Hunter doesn't mean I should have looked there.

The crunch of gravel gets my attention. A jolt of panic shoots up my spine.

They're here.

Fifteen minutes early. That's fine. The sooner we get this over with, the better.

Two cars pull into the lot, both dark sedans, and park on either side of me. I strain to get a visual of Brady, but I don't see him. Where is he? The drivers are easy enough to make out, and there's a passenger in one of the cars, but he's clearly not Brady. More panic as various scenarios flow through my mind. Is Brady tied up in the back seat? Is he in the trunk? *Please let him be okay.*

Just open the door and step out of my car. *No sudden moves.* My trembling hands grip the steering wheel as I make eye contact with each of the drivers. Deep breath. *You can do this.* With slow and steady movements, I exit the car and walk to meet the two men now waiting for me at the back of my car.

I'm not sure what I was expecting, but this isn't it. They look like normal people. Both are in their thirties, although one of them does seem a couple years older than the other. They both have brown eyes and short, brown hair. They're average height, average build, average everything. They do kind of look alike. Maybe they're brothers or cousins or something. I don't recall ever seeing either of them before, but then I'm not exactly a local anymore.

Be confident.

"Where's my brother?"

"He's safe. Hand over the bag." The younger one takes it from me before I can even comply with the order. "Is it all here?"

"Yes. Now, where's Brady?"

"We'll take you to him."

Um, no. No way.

"That wasn't the deal. I retrieved the bag. Now give me my brother."

The older one smirks, his eyes gleam. "She's feisty. I like that."

Bile works its way up my throat. I swallow hard to keep it down, although I don't know why. He deserves a lot worse than me throwing up on his shoes.

"Get in the car."

A gun. The younger one has a gun in his hand.

Why didn't I ask Hunter for help?

Hunter.

Why am I thinking about Hunter at a time like this?

The older guy grabs my arm and pulls me toward one of the cars. He opens the door and stares at me with his hard eyes.

So stupid.

With no other choice, I climb into the back seat. The brother with the gun gets in on the other side. And just like that, we're driving away from Pigeon Park. The other car that came with them follows us out.

They make no effort to cover my eyes. Aren't they supposed to do that? Does that mean that they plan to kill me? What if Brady's already dead? Tears fill my eyes. *I can't go down like this.* What are my options?

"Where are you taking me?"

"To your brother. Just like we said."

Chapter Twelve

Hunter

What is she doing?

"Don't get in the car!"

The words are nothing more than a heavy whisper, an attempt to will Kate away from these men, but I know that it doesn't work like that. She's being held at gunpoint. Why didn't she talk to me? We could have figured out whatever this is. I could have helped her.

I knew that Kate was up to something, and I should have made an attempt to stop her. I should have made her tell me. I just never guessed it was anything this dangerous.

It's too late to stop her from meeting these men,

but I'll be damned if I'm going to let them hurt her. I don't have the right firearm for any accuracy at this distance, and there's no point in firing to scare them. They might hurt her, and once they know I'm here, I won't have a chance to save her. Or Brady for that matter.

They didn't shoot her on the spot. They want her alive for some reason, that, or they don't want to do it here. Just the thought leaves me dizzy.

My binoculars provide a good view of them down below. The driveway of an abandoned farmhouse makes a good hiding place. I'll do my best to follow them. These winding roads are not ideal for the task, but I won't stop until I find Kate.

The two cars pull away from the small lot and turn in my direction. I duck down in my Jeep for good measure. Thank goodness I opted for the green Jeep. I almost went for the bright yellow one, and that would have stood out like a sore thumb.

My call connects to dispatch as the two cars pass the end of the driveway. The operator takes my information and then patches me through to the chief himself. Chief Tisdale is off today as well, but he'll be working now after all. He won't let a rescue like this go down in his jurisdiction without him.

I give the cars a twenty-second head start and pull onto the road behind them. The rolling hills are a distinct disadvantage when trying to follow. I have to be far enough behind so they don't see me crest the hill, but close enough that I'll be able to see if they make any turns. Fortunately, there aren't a lot of turns to be made on this particular road, and I manage to catch a glimpse of them making a right turn. I relay the information to the operator and keep my eyes peeled for any other moves.

Kate must be so scared. *Please, God. Let her be okay.* You finally brought her back into my life. I can't lose her again.

We travel another two miles together before I lose sight of the vehicles. It's a gamble now. Did they speed up and get far enough ahead that I can't see them, or did they turn? I go with my gut and turn around. There are four driveways between my current location and the last place the cars were spotted. Two of the driveways lead to homes that can be seen from the road. The cars parked out in front of them are not the ones I was following, so that leaves two choices. I make the first left and drive slowly down the leaf and snow-covered driveway. It's barely a path that's been cut through the trees, so it's easy to keep hidden. I just hope they don't hear my approach. If they do, I'm screwed.

The driveway ends at a run-down shack that's being taken over by nature. There are no cars and nowhere else to hide. I quickly turn around and speed down the path back to the main road. There's only one more place that they can be. Of course it's the old Franklin place. How many times did I have to drive there to pick up my dad when he was incapacitated? *Don't think about that now.*

I pray to God that I'm in the right place and that reinforcements aren't far behind. There's no time to wait.

Chapter Thirteen

Kate

The clock on the dash shows that we've been riding for twelve minutes, but it feels like the longest drive of my life. The man next to me hasn't taken his eyes or the aim of his gun off me. It's strange. He really does seem totally normal. He wears khakis and a navy ski jacket. He looks like he came here straight from the country club or something. What kind of criminals wear khakis?

We pull onto a thin, dirt road. The bumpiness of it is a big change from the smooth highway. My already nervous stomach again threatens release. I hug my stomach, swallow hard, and close my eyes until the car comes to a stop. Now what happens?

My door opens. The brothers haven't moved. This must be the other driver. I step out cautiously to find another gun pointed at me. There's no chance of escape at this point. I take in what I can of my surroundings. Maybe I'll have a chance to escape later. *Please.*

We're at a farm. It doesn't look the least bit familiar, just a typical farmhouse. A front porch extends across the entire front of the structure and wraps around the back side. The house is painted blue, or maybe I should say it was painted blue. Much of the paint is worn and faded. There's a barn that's even larger than the house and another smaller outbuilding. Both are pretty run down.

The brothers joins us. *Fantastic, now I have two guns pointed at me.*

"Let's get moving." The third guy motions toward the house with the barrel of his gun.

This is a really bad idea, but I have no choice. The older brother gives me a nudge, and I start walking.

"Brady!"

"Kate!"

The relief I feel at seeing my brother is indescribable...and he's alive. Both his hands and his feet are bound to the chair in which he sits with some type of zip ties. A dark bruise rings his right eye. *Please don't let anything else be hurt.* A fresh round of tears starts. I step toward Brady, but they pull me back and then plop me down into my own chair on the other side of the room. *Fight. Do...not... let them do this.* Each of the brothers holds one of my arms against those of the chair. I pull against them, but even though it takes some effort on their part, they hold firm. The movements only cause pain for me as my arms are pressed even harder against the wooden chair

The third man threads a tie around my right wrist and pulls until the band of plastic presses against my skin. Pain shoots up my arm. I cry out and kick my leg upward. It connects with the shin of the third man. He falls to the side uttering an obscenity but quickly rights himself.

"You bitch." With fire in his eyes, he moves his hand back to hit me. One of the brothers grabs his arm as it heads toward my face.

"Don't hurt her!" Brady's screams go ignored. I appreciate the effort, but there's nothing he can do to help me right now.

"No way," the older brother lectures. "This isn't what we need to be doing right now. We need to focus on the job. You will have plenty of time later to show her who's boss."

The third guy says nothing else to me, but the look in his eyes says plenty. His grimace morphs into a sinister smile. I swallow hard. *Please don't let him get a chance to do whatever it is he wants to do to me.*

The zip of the second tie brings me back to my current situation, but it's too late. The tie tears at the already tender flesh of my wrist. I kick my legs again, but now that my arms are secured, they focus their efforts on my legs, easily strapping them to the legs of the chair.

The younger brother places the cosmetic bag on the end of the large farmhouse table, and the three men begin going through the contents. It's the first real chance I've had to study the third man, the one who must have been driving the other car. He's not a relative, at least he doesn't look anything like the other two guys. He's older, probably in his mid-thirties, and he has fair hair and blue eyes. For what it's worth, he doesn't look like a criminal either. Apparently, they come in all shapes and sizes and look nothing like the dark characters on television.

Diamonds are dumped from the powder canister —knew about that one—the blush, and the eyeshadow. When they are finished going through each of the make-up items, they cut open the bag itself. One look at Brady and his wide eyes, and I know that he knew nothing about the diamonds.

The older guy reaches toward me, grabs a fistful of my hair, and yanks. A yelp escapes as fireworks flash into my vision.

"Where are the rest?"

What rest? My eyes meet his, hard and unyielding. "I don't know what you mean. I brought you the bag just like it was."

"You kept some for yourself first, ten to be exact."

This is very bad. A faintness passes over me. Whatever breaths I can manage aren't deep enough to get the much-needed oxygen into my lungs.

Do not pass out.

"No."

"You did, and you're going to tell me what you did with them."

"Leave her alone!"

Brady's shout does nothing other than bring a smile to the man's lips. He leans forward, his body way too close to mine, and whispers in my ear. "I'm glad you're spunky. This is going to be fun."

His words and the heat of his breath cause me to gag.

Keep it together. Do not let him scare you.

Easier said than done. Panic is close.

"Get away from her!" Brady screams at them as he shakes in his chair in an effort to escape his bindings.

Shots ring out in the little room.

The man cries out in pain and drops to the floor next to me.

"What the fuck?" the younger man screams, his words loud even over the wailing of the man who's been shot. His hands move toward the gun tucked in his pants. Too late. He falls as well. The third guy holds his hands up, doesn't even fight back. My eyes search frantically for the source of the bullets.

Hunter.

He comes to me at a run. There are others here, too. The scene is chaotic as men run in from the front and back of the house yelling orders. The brothers lie on the floor screaming. It's all background noise. My eyes are on Hunter.

He cuts my bindings and pulls me to him. Waves of relief flow over me, leaving me weak and dizzy. He's here. He saved us.

He leans back and looks into my eyes. *Those eyes.*

"Katie."

Both his hands move to cup my chin. He pulls me even closer, our foreheads touch as he caresses my cheeks with his thumbs. Our breath mixes and mingles.

This is it.

He's going to kiss me.

My lips open in anticipation.

Hunter steps back, and just like before, the magic of the moment is gone. All the blood in my body rushes to my head. The effects are dizzying, making me grab the chair for support.

Hunter steps closer and gingerly touches my shoulder.

"Did they hurt you?"

"No." *You did, you moron.* I swallow heavily in an effort to dislodge the enormous knot in my throat. "I'm fine."

He gives me a strange look and then moves across the room to speak to one of his colleagues. *Jerk.*

"Kate, I'm so sorry that I got you involved in this."

Brady. I pull him to me for a hug. He's alive. I'm alive. That's all that matters.

"What is this? How did *you* get involved?"

His blue eyes show his sadness. Brady's one year older than I am, Irish twins, as they say. We look like twin-twins and have always been as close. The year never made much of a difference. In fact, there were many times when people thought I was older, simply because I had always been the more mature one. The whole *girls mature faster than boys* thing is proven with us.

"Jamie asked me to help her. I don't know much more than that. I didn't know that there were diamonds. I'm just so glad that you're okay. I'm so sorry." He pulls me to him again.

"Jamie, the woman you've been dating? That Jamie?"

"Yeah."

What the hell is she involved in?

EMTs enter and kneel down by the screaming brothers. A much older man wearing a black vest surveys the room. *Chief Tisdale*. Our eyes meet as he walks over to me, a smile on his face. He has a nice smile that goes well with his soft gray eyes and short, gray hair. He's a bit on the portly side, but nothing crazy. He just looks like his wife is a good cook, probably because she is. I haven't seen the Tisdales in years, but they are both regulars at my parent's store. The chief has a fondness for candied orange slices.

"Kate Richardson." I nod and attempt a smile. The lump in my throat is smaller but still in the way. "So glad that we were here in time to help you and Brady, but as you can imagine, we have a lot of questions for you. Will you be okay to accompany us back to the station?"

"Yes, sir."

"Officer McMann will drive you. Or, would you be more comfortable with Officer Simms?"

Hunter turns toward me at the sound of his name. "No. Officer McMann is good." *Great even.*

Chief Tisdale motions a man over.

"McMann, this is Miss Kate Richardson."

Officer McMann is a bit older than I am, and he is good looking. He's about six feet tall, about two inches shorter than Hunter. He has the look of a surfer with blond, wavy hair, large blue eyes, and a face that looks like it's been chiseled from marble. He's tan even. Does he go to the tanning salon, or is it left over from the summer? Hunter would never go to a tanning place.

Why am I comparing Officer McMann to Hunter? Probably because I compare every man to Hunter. I always have, even when I don't mean to. No one kisses like Hunter. No one makes me feel as secure as Hunter. And no one makes me as crazy as Hunter.

I sneak a look in his direction. He's watching us. Officer McMann extends his arm toward me, and I take it. I've given Hunter every sign that I like him, and he isn't getting it. Or worse, Hunter gets it, and he's not interested. Maybe some good, old-fashioned jealousy will work. My arm moves around that of Officer McMann, and I let him escort me out of the house. Sure, I could walk without his support, but it's nice to have someone to lean on after all I've been through.

Officer McMann gets me settled in the front seat of his Ford Fusion before excusing himself for a moment. I watch as he returns to the house, and I take in the scene outside. The kidnappers who were injured are being loaded into ambulances. The older man was shot in the shoulder, the younger one in the leg. Both are talking to the paramedics, so although they are most definitely hurting, it doesn't seem critical. That's a good thing, too. They need to be able to talk so that we can figure out what's happening.

Hunter exits the house with Chief Tisdale. The third criminal walks between them, his wrists restrained behind his back. Hunter's eyes find mine. He tips his head in apology. Don't ask me how I know that he's sorry just from this gesture, but I do. For what, I'm not exactly sure. Because he held me so tightly? Because he let me go so easily? *Be reasonable.* Maybe he was embarrassed for grabbing me like that in front of his co-workers. We aren't dating. We aren't even friends. My anger begins to soften. *Geez, Hunter.* I can't even stay mad at you anymore.

I don't want to.

The car door opens behind me, and Brady climbs into the backseat. Dark circles line his eyes, even where he doesn't have the shiner. He sighs heavily and lays his head back on the seat. Officer McMann climbs into the driver's seat, and we're off.

"How long did they have you?"

"They got me on my way to work yesterday. I was only about a block from my house. They pinned me in with their cars. Before I even knew what was happening, they had a gun in my face. There was nowhere to go."

"Oh, Brady."

"You knew something was up by then, right? Why didn't you go see Hunter right away? Why did you plan to wait until dinner time?"

He shrugs. His eyes are wet with tears. "I didn't know that it was so serious. All I knew up until that point was that Jamie asked me to hide something for her, and then she disappeared."

"When did you last speak with her?"

"She stayed over at my place on Wednesday night. She came straight to see me from the airport. Everything was normal on Thursday morning. She left as if she was going to work. Then she called my office around noon on Thursday. She explained that she'd left her make-up bag in my bathroom. I already knew that she'd left it—she often forgot things at my place—so that part wasn't a surprise. The part that was a surprise was that she asked me to hide it for her. I mean, why would she want to keep make-up hidden?"

"You didn't ask her what was so important about a bag of make-up?"

"No, I didn't ask. I figured I was missing something, so I drove home at lunch to check it out. It was just make-up. But, she did ask me to hide it for her, so I did. She asked me to hide the bag someplace where no one would know to look. A vision of our fort popped into my head. It seemed silly. I hadn't been up there in over a month, so I thought it was worth checking out—two birds with one stone kind of thing. I drove up to the cabin during my lunch hour and left the bag in our treasure chest. Jamie called me Thursday night and asked me if I'd hidden the bag. I assured her that it was in a safe place, and that was it. I haven't spoken with her since."

"Did you tell the police?"

"I was going to talk to Hunter about it. I wasn't really sure what to do. Jamie and I have only been dating a month. It was a weird request, but I don't know her habits. It's bizarre, but it isn't illegal to hide your make-up." Makes sense I guess. "I drove up to her place on Thursday night. No one answered the door, and her car wasn't there. I was disappointed that I couldn't see her but planned to call her sometime Friday morning."

Officer McMann looks at me with kind eyes. He hasn't interrupted our conversation, but he's listening for sure. We're almost to town, and then we'll be going over our stories over and over, I'm certain. It was dark when I drove through last night on the way to the cabin—dark, snowing, and sleeting. My senses were on high alert, on the lookout for Mom, Dad, or some other family member who would report the sighting to my parents. This was supposed to be a stealth mission. Get in, save Brady, and get out before they knew that he was in trouble. That totally backfired.

Davidson, Virginia is a fairly small town, smack in the middle of the state, about twenty miles south of Charlottesville. We have a real downtown area, a few restaurants, and even a Wal-Mart. It's big enough so that everyone doesn't know everyone, but you do know a pretty good percentage of the people who live here. It helps that my family runs a staple of the town, the Richardson General Store. My family has owned the store for more than one hundred years. They sell just about everything, but the best part, and the reason people come from miles around, is the soda fountain and the penny candy. My parents run the store now. They had hoped that Brady would take over, but he's a computer programmer.

Officer McMann pulls into the small lot adjacent to the police station and cuts the engine. My parent's store is only a block away. Brady and I both stare in that direction as we walk inside. Like what, our parents are going to be outside on the sidewalk waiting to catch us? Probably not, but neither of us dilly-dally. We're both close to thirty, and we're worried about our parents catching us. Does the fear of disappointing your parents ever go away?

The reception area is small with just enough room for a counter with a desk behind it and a waiting area. I've been here before, but this is the first time I've been here for any kind of trouble. I've always been a good girl. No one sits behind the desk today. Dottie Matheson normally sits there, but it's Saturday, so she has the day off.

Officer McMann escorts us to a cozy seating area to the side comprised of a couch and two chairs and then leaves to get us some coffee. Something warm would be very nice and might stop my shivering. It's probably caused by adrenaline this time, but it's worth a try. Brady puts his arm around me, and I lean my head on his shoulder.

I'm not upset with Brady for calling me. If he's in trouble, then I want to help him. Of course, it would be nice if he didn't associate with women involved in diamond theft.

"How did Jamie end up with the diamonds?"

"I don't know how she got them. I need to find her. She's in trouble."

My forehead wrinkles. "She knows that. She knew she was putting you in danger when she gave you that bag to hide. I mean, come on."

"And then I put you in danger. I'm sorry, Kate."

"Brady, please come with us. We need to ask you

a few questions." Chief Tisdale walks into the room. "We'll be with you soon, Kate."

Brady gives my shoulder a squeeze, stands, and follows the police chief toward the back of the building, leaving me alone with my thoughts.

Chapter Fourteen

Hunter

It's great when criminals carry their driver's licenses on them. Makes the job of identifying them so much easier. We will verify their identities, but it's still a time saver. David William Justice is now booked and behind bars. The FBI has been contacted, and agents are on their way from Charlottesville. The chief is questioning Brady. It's a good time to check on Kate. I even make a trip to Leslie's sandwich shop for a peace offering.

"Kate?" She opens her eyes slowly and looks at me. *Thank you, God, for letting her be okay.* "Are you hungry?" I place the take-out container on the table in front of her. "Turkey sandwich from Leslie's. It's the fanciest lunch I could think of."

She lifts the lid and looks inside. "It looks great. Thank you, but why do you think I need a fancy lunch?"

"You have fancy recipes on your blog, so I was just trying to give you something to make up for the cold pizza you had for breakfast."

"You've read my blog?"

Busted.

"Yeah. You're kind of famous around here, a local celebrity and all." Kate looks down at her lap as her blush travels up her cheeks.

Deep breath. My hands itch to touch her—to hold her and tell her that everything is going to be okay. Instead, I take a seat in the chair across from her and watch my hands as they grip the armrests.

Stop stalling, and spit it out.

"I want to ask you a favor. I understand if you don't want to, and I have no right to ask." My gaze rises to meet hers. "We don't know how big this operation is, and it's likely that we don't have everyone involved behind bars. We don't have Jamie and there are likely others. So..." *Spit it out.* "I would feel much better if you and Brady would stay with me until this is over." Kate opens her mouth to respond. She's going to argue with me. I don't give her the chance. "And I'm sorry for getting carried away when we found you. You don't know how scared I was when I saw them take you."

"You followed me?"

"I did. I could tell that you were hiding something, and I knew that it had something to do with Brady's disappearance. You didn't just fly to Virginia on a whim when you'll be here next week anyway. I knew that Brady wouldn't ditch me without a phone call. Plus, you never tried to call Brady from the cabin, and you didn't seem surprised that I hadn't heard from him. You knew he was in trouble. Why didn't you ask me for help?"

"They said that I wasn't to tell anyone, that they would kill him if law enforcement got involved. I was scared."

"I know."

The need to pull her against me is overwhelming. I close my eyes until the urge subsides. Holding Kate is heaven and hell all at once. It's a promise of the wonders of what could be and a taste of something that I can't have. I can't keep doing this to myself.

"So, will you stay at my house?"

"Okay. Just for one night. I'm going home tomorrow. Wait, can I go home tomorrow?"

No. Davidson is your home. This is where you belong. "I don't know yet. We'll see what the chief says, and the FBI agents when they get here."

Kate's eyes widen at the mention of FBI. Normally I'd be ticked that they were coming in to take over the investigation, but in this case, I'm okay with it. I'll still know what's going on, and I will have the time I need to make sure that Kate and Brady stay out of harm's way. Kate's staying with me though, and that's the first step to keeping her safe.

"Your parents are going to hear about this soon. You know what the grapevine is like around here. Why don't we walk down to the store so they can see that you're really okay?"

Her nose crinkles. "Can I just call them?"

My lip curls up into a smile. First, Kate's freckles look adorable when she grimaces, and second, because there's no way her parents are going for just a phone call. There's no point, they'd be down here in two seconds. Kate knows that, too. She sighs a heavy sigh and brings her bottom lip up into a pout. *Those lips. I almost kissed her back at that house.* Then what would I have done?

Smile gone. My fingers curl tighter into the fabric of the chair.

"Alright. Let's go."

Kate stands too quickly and then wobbles a bit before steadying herself. A gentleman would offer her his arm, just like McMann did back at the farm house. *Gosh, that burned me up.* But, what the hell can I do about it? I don't trust myself to touch her.

"Are you okay to walk? Do you want to eat something first?"

She smiles a nervous smile. "I don't want to eat yet. I don't know what that was. I'm okay."

She's not okay, and I'm an asshole. I shove my

hands into my pockets and follow Kate out the front door of the station. We walk in silence down the sidewalk toward her family's store. The afternoon sun is warm, melting the snow and ice at a record pace. There's hardly any left.

"I bet it was fun growing up with your family owning a store like they do."

Her eyes meet mine as she brushes a stray lock of hair behind her ear. "It was great. It's a miracle that Brady and I both don't weigh four hundred pounds."

"Too much free candy?"

She smiles as she recalls some good memories. "Yeah. Mom finally had to ration it out. I still love going in there and watching the kids' faces light up as they look at the candy aisle."

"I know mine did."

We're here. The big glass display windows are decorated with everything Thanksgiving. Pots and pans, dish towels, spatulas, and a huge plush turkey.

"That's Fred."

"What?"

"The turkey. We've had him since Brady and I were little. He makes his appearance every November, the day after Halloween to be exact. Brady named him Fred." With a deep breath, she opens the door. "Here we go."

Chapter Fifteen

Kate

Just walking through the door brings back so many wonderful memories. Dad lifts his head at the chime of the bells. His eyes widen in surprise when he sees me. What do I even say to them?

"Kate!" He rounds the counter and pulls me to him for a tight hug. "Gracie! You're not going to believe this. Kate's home."

Mom is here now, too, hugging me tightly. I breathe in the scent of the store. Cinnamon and powdered sugar. Nothing else smells so good. A few customers pop their heads up to see what all the commotion is about and then quickly decide I'm not worth their time.

Mom holds both my hands in hers and studies me. I'm wearing the same clothes that I traveled in yesterday and no make-up at all. I'm also still wearing Mom's boots and coat that I borrowed from the cabin this morning.

"What's going on?"

How exactly do I tell her that her son is somehow involved with a jewel heist or diamond smuggling? Who knows?

"Albert, Grace, would it be okay if we speak somewhere alone?"

"Hi there, Hunter. Of course we can."

Mom looks quickly from Hunter to me and then back to Hunter but doesn't comment on the fact that I showed up in her store with someone that she thinks I hate. Big sigh. Hunter sure doesn't feel like an enemy anymore. I can hardly believe that I ever thought he was.

Dad ushers us into the back room. The room is small already and crammed with overstock that doesn't fit in the storage room. It's a tight fit for the four of us.

"Tell me what's going on." Mom speaks to Hunter directly, since I ignored her the first time.

"Everything is just fine. Both Kate and Brady are okay."

"Brady?" Mom says his name in a squeak and turns to me. I feel the heat of her gaze as her eyes scan me like an x-ray, checking for breaks or who knows what. It's her mom vision.

"I'm fine, Mom. Really."

"And where is Brady?"

Hunter reaches out and touches Mom's shoulder. "Brady's talking with Chief Tisdale to try to figure out what happened. See, he was kidnapped yesterday."

"What! Why? Who would do something like that?"

"We have three men in custody. All we know at this point is that it has something to do with his girlfriend, Jamie."

"That can't be right. Jamie is a sweet young woman. She can't be involved in anything shady."

My gaze moves from Mom to Hunter, and a silent communication passes between us. We've said enough.

"We are investigating to see what happened."

Mom nods. "That doesn't explain why you're here?"

"Brady called me yesterday and asked me to come. He said that he needed my help with something."

"How was he taken? Did they hurt him in any way?"

"He has a bruise under his eye, but he is fine otherwise."

"I want to see that for myself. I'm going down there." Mom begins to walk toward the door. I hold out my hand to halt her.

"He really is fine. I promise. They took him to an

old farmhouse and tied him to a chair."

Mom eyes me skeptically. She pulls her cell phone out of her pocket and begins pecking on it, calling Brady, I imagine.

"Is it true that you were kidnapped?" Mom's voice is a higher pitch than usual. Her gaze is on me again as if to let me know that she's checking out my story. It's like the time I told her that I went on a church retreat, and she called to verify my attendance. I was in huge trouble that day because, in actuality, Melanie and I skipped the retreat and went to the lake instead. I should have made Brady come with us. I should have known that Mom would be like this. "I see. And you're sure that you're okay? As soon as you're finished with the sheriff, you need to come down here to the store. I have to see you with my own two eyes." She nods slightly as she disconnects. I know better than to say *I told you so*. "How long will you be able to stay in Davidson? Can you just stay until after Thanksgiving? Surely you can be away for two weeks."

Another look at Hunter. His eyes are gray and thoughtful, but they give away no clue as to what's happening in there.

"I'm not sure how long I'll be staying. Chief Tisdale is supposed to let me know when I can leave."

"Grace, maybe you have some house projects that Kate can work on for material for her blog. That way she can stay here in town and still get some work done."

The wattage of Mom's smile increases to blinding. *Thanks a lot, Hunter*. It's not that I don't want to help Mom with her projects, but using my mother to make me stay in town is a low blow. If staying in Davidson is going to mean sparring back and forth with Hunter the whole time, then maybe I don't want to stay after all. And I agreed to stay at his house. Why did I do that? One look at Mom, and I know that it's too late to get out of this. I'm staying.

"Ooh! I've been hoping to freshen up my kitchen. I was going to ask you about it when you came home anyway. This way, we can work on it together." Mom steps toward me for another hug. "This is great. You can stay for two weeks. Winston will be so excited."

Winston is their liver and white cocker spaniel. He does like me, but I think he likes anyone who feeds him table scraps. Besides, I didn't say I was staying.

And there's more news to tell her. Not sure which way to go with my other news. If I tell my parents that Brady and I are staying with Hunter, then they will be suspicious right away that we aren't safe. If I tell them that I'm staying with Hunter, it will be total shock and awe, but they'll think it's for reasons other than my safety. That will be a lot to deal with, but I can deal with it later.

"We'll see, Mom. There's something else, too. I'm going to be staying at Hunter's house, at least for tonight."

"Really?" Her jaw drops to the floor. Normally, nothing surprises this woman. She looks back and forth between us. Hunter seems to be blushing. I know I am. "When did this happen?"

"Nothing has happened, Mom." *Unfortunately*. "Hunter offered, and I accepted. That's it."

"I see." Her mind is working a mile a minute. "You'll both come to lunch tomorrow, yes?"

"Yes, ma'am." Hunter speaks quickly. "Kate, we need to be getting back."

I kiss them both on the cheek and follow Hunter outside. His skin is still at least one shade redder than normal.

FBI Special Agents Cole and Rodriguez are waiting in the lobby area when we return. Both shake hands with Hunter as if they know him already and then shake hands with me. They seem nice enough. Agent Rodriguez is in his fifties. He's African American with a bald or possibly shaved head. Agent Cole is probably mid-thirties with dark brown hair. His brown eyes are kind, but his mannerisms are all business.

"We have a few questions for you, Ms. Richardson."

"Of course."

"Ms. Richardson hasn't eaten her lunch yet. Would it be okay with you if she eats while you talk to her?"

"No problem at all. Why don't we just have a seat over here?"

We all get settled in the reception area. I take my original spot. Hunter sits beside me. Agent Cole begins the questioning while I dig into my sandwich. It's three o'clock, and I'm starving. Anything from Leslie's promises to be delicious, and this sandwich is no exception: turkey, Havarti, and some kind of dill spread. Delicious.

"So, Ms. Richardson. When did you first hear from Brady?"

"Yesterday morning. He called me around eight o'clock my time. I live in Austin, Texas. He sounded nervous, and I knew that something was wrong right away."

"What did he say?"

"Brady said that it was a life or death emergency and that he needed me to do something for him. He asked me to retrieve a bag from our treasure box and bring it to Pigeon Park at one o'clock today."

"Did you find the request odd?"

"Yes. For sure. Brady and I haven't spoken of our treasure box in years. Plus, if Brady needed something from our treasure box, why wouldn't he get it himself? Why did I have to fly all the way here to take care of it? I mean, I know that he and I are the only ones who know what that means, but even now, why didn't he just take the criminals there himself?"

"He told us that he didn't want them to know about your family's cabin."

"I guess I get that, but they're awfully patient criminals to wait more than twenty-four hours for their diamonds."

"Agreed. So, what did you do?"

"Exactly what Brady asked. I threw some things into a bag and went to the airport. I was able to get on the one-thirty flight. The plane ticket cost me a fortune, but I knew that Brady would pay me back."

"What time did you land?"

"Five-thirty at Dulles. Not fun. D.C. rush hour sucks. It started snowing before I got out of town. The weather just got worse and worse. I didn't get to Davidson until close to nine-thirty. I didn't want anyone to know that I was in town, so I tried to make it to the cabin. The mountain road was treacherous, but I had nowhere else to go. I had to get to the cabin. My rental, however, was not designed for ice and got stuck. I walked the rest of the way. Well, most of it, anyway. Hunter heard me outside the cabin and came out to find me."

All eyes turn to Hunter. His tone is all business as he answers. "I have a personal friendship with Brady Richardson. He called me yesterday morning and asked me to meet him at the cabin for dinner. He said that he needed to talk to me about something."

"What time was that?"

"Six-thirty, earlier than when he called Kate. It was before he was taken."

"So, you were there at the cabin waiting for Brady to arrive?"

"I was, but the storm really kicked in around eight. Once it really got going, I didn't expect Brady to make it. I started to worry as time went on and he hadn't called me. He hadn't even called to say he would be late, and he's normally very conscientious about that kind of thing."

"Did you know that Ms. Richardson was coming to the cabin?"

"No idea." Hunter doesn't look at me. He keeps his focus on the agents across from us. "It was close to eleven when Kate arrived at the cabin. I was still awake. I heard a noise and found Kate when I went out to investigate."

And he held me in his arms and carried me into the cabin. My throat tightens.

"Then what happened?"

"We compared notes. Somewhat anyway. Kate told me about Brady's phone call and her trip to Virginia, but she didn't tell me the reason that she came. The next morning she was acting funny. She *went for a hike*." Hunter uses his fingers to quote the words as he speaks. "I could tell that she had something hidden in her jacket when she returned, but I didn't ask about it."

"Why not?"

"Kate and I haven't always gotten along,"— *understatement*—"and I knew that she wouldn't confide in me. So, I let her think that I hadn't noticed how strangely she was acting, and then, when we left, I followed her."

Agent Rodriguez smiles. "You didn't think that would piss her off."

Hunter shrugs. "I figured if she was really up to nothing, then it wouldn't matter. But, it turns out that it's a good thing I did."

"Definitely. Under normal circumstances, I would have been mad that Hunter followed me, but considering what happened, thank goodness he did." Hunter meets my gaze for a quick second and then looks back at the agents.

"I watched Kate as she waited down at Pigeon Park. As soon as the two men got out of their cars, I knew something bad was going to happen. I was at too great a distance to do anything then, so I followed them back to the farmhouse. That's where they were holding Brady."

"Ms. Richardson, what happened when the men came to the park?"

"I had the bag that they wanted. I was naive enough to think that they would just trade me the bag for Brady like they had promised." My eyes are wet now. I swallow and clear my throat to keep my voice steady. "I don't know why I thought that. I was so focused on getting Brady back that I didn't really think about anything else." *Well, I did think a lot about Hunter, but the FBI doesn't need to know that.*

"I looked in the bag and saw some of the diamonds in the loose powder canister. I knew then that I should have asked Hunter for help, but it was too late. The two men who look like brothers got out of the cars. One of them had a gun and made me go with them. They drove me to the farmhouse. We were only there a little bit before the police showed up. They had just started yelling at me, saying that I didn't bring them all the diamonds."

"How many are missing?"

"Ten. That's what they said anyway."

"Officer Simms, let's go have a pow-wow with the chief to see where we go from here. If you don't mind waiting here, Ms. Richardson, we'll be right back with you."

All three men stand and walk quietly into the back. I finish off my sandwich, pondering all the questions I have for Brady. My spirits rise when he walks back in just a few moments later.

"Tell them that I promise I'll be back to answer their questions." His eyes are a little wild. "I have to find Jamie. She's in danger."

I stand and walk toward him. Unfortunately for Brady, we're both about the same height. He's five-foot-nine, and I'm only two inches shorter.

"Are you out of your mind? Did Chief Tisdale tell you that you can leave?" He doesn't answer, but it's easy to see that he's sneaking out. "They can help you find her. Hunter is your best friend—something that you forgot to tell me apparently—he'll help you. We can go to Hunter's house together and figure out a plan. That's *after* you go see Mom and Dad."

"I have to find her."

Brady walks out the front door before I have a chance to argue.

"Where's Brady?"

Hunter and Officer McMann stand in the doorway. Hunter knows that Brady bailed. I can tell by the tone of his voice.

"He said that he had to find Jamie."

Hunter's displeasure is written all over his face. "Sonofabitch. He doesn't listen for shit."

I shrug. It's true.

Officer McMann doesn't appear nearly as bothered by Brady's defection. "We brought your rental car here to the station, but we'd like to keep it until at least tomorrow." *Great.* "Can I give you a ride to your parents' house? Is that where you're staying?"

"She's staying with me."

Officer McMann starts in surprise. It's not so much the words that Hunter spoke, but how he said them—his voice extra deep as if he's marking me as his property or something. I should be ticked off, but instead my stomach quivers. Now, if the rest of Hunter would get with the program.

Chief Tisdale and the FBI agents join us. We go over my story two more times. Officer McMann's eyes shine with understanding when he learns that

Hunter and I spent the night together last night. It wasn't romantic in any way, but it could have been if the details are left to the imagination—people jump to their own conclusions. It is a surprise that I'm wishing it had been a romantic evening. The conditions were sure right for it. Maybe I hit my head when I fell last night, and this is all a dream. While I forgave Hunter years ago, it's still difficult to imagine us as a couple. *A couple?* Now I'm really getting ahead of myself.

Hunter produces my purse and my carry-on bag when it's time to leave the station. Such a relief that my purse was still in my car. I won't be able to fly home without my driver's license.

The drive to Hunter's home is completely silent. He keeps his eyes straight ahead on the road in front of us, his jaw set. I study him whenever I can sneak a look without staring. I admit it to myself—I'm way nervous. It isn't that I'm afraid something will happen between us. I'm afraid that something won't. This trip has taught me that I *want* to get to know him better. I want Hunter to want me, too. So far, he's a mystery.

Chapter Sixteen

Hunter

How thick is the layer of dust on the coffee table? How many dirty dishes are in the sink? What is Kate going to think of my boring, little house? She decorates for a living. She's going to think it's horrible.

Did I pick up the dirty clothes off my bedroom floor? *That doesn't matter.* Kate isn't going in my bedroom.

This is impossible. I was an idiot to think that I could pull this off. What did I think would happen? It's true that I want to keep Kate safe. My intentions are good. That has to count for something. If I'm honest with myself, is that all I want?

Yes. She's only going to lead to trouble.

I pull my Jeep into its usual spot, next to the house. Does Kate have a house in Austin? A tidy garage and an automatic opener? I park on a patch of dirt. With a deep breath, I take in the view of my house and imagine what it looks like through Kate's eyes. It isn't horrible. It's a single story house with a long front porch. I've done so much work on this house in the last ten years that it feels like I've replaced just about every board in the place. The problem is that it's boring. Kennedy wanted to plant flowers on either side of the steps, but I wouldn't let her spend the money. It just gets worse on the inside. Kate won't be impressed with boring, white walls.

But, I'm not trying to impress her.

I'm trying to keep her out of harm's way. That's all that matters.

Kate's eyes are busily taking it all in.

"It isn't much."

She turns to me and smiles. "It's great. I love the exposed wood beams on the porch. Did you do this yourself?" She rubs her hand on the log railing. I nod. "Great work. These chairs are amazing, too. Where did you get them?"

"I made those, too."

"I didn't know you worked with wood. You're really talented."

This is going to be hard.

"Come on inside. I'll show you to your room."

Kate follows me into the living room, and I brace myself for impact. My eyes dart around the room to pick out everything that's out of place. A coffee cup and two glasses are on the coffee table. The quilt isn't folded, but it's never folded, so I can't expect that to magically happen. No dirty clothes on the floor. It isn't as bad as it could have been, that's for sure.

"Did you refinish these floors, too? They're beautiful." They did turn out pretty good, but that wasn't hard. "And that fireplace. Wow."

The fireplace opening is larger than most. The stone base is wide and takes up most of the wall, floor to ceiling. It's always been my favorite thing about this house.

"I love that you've kept it wood-burning and didn't install gas logs."

My heart flips in my chest. Does she know that's exactly how I feel about it? *Put some distance between yourself and her...now.*

"Let me show you to Kennedy's room. That's where you'll be sleeping."

"Where is Kennedy going to sleep?"

"Kennedy doesn't technically live here anymore. She moved in with our granny last year."

Kate follows me down the small hallway. "Kennedy likes color. We painted her room pink when she turned sixteen. It's the only room that isn't white, so you'll be more comfortable here."

"Your house is great, Hunter." She touches my

forearm. The electricity zings from my elbow to my shoulder. "There are so many unique touches that you don't usually see. Sure, you could use a coat of paint, but that's nothing. Throw pillows aren't for everyone."

"No throw pillows allowed." She smiles again, and this time, so do I.

"Can I take a shower?"

"Of course. There's only one bathroom, but you can have it first. Right here across the hall." The bathroom is a mess. I gather my toiletries together in a corner of the vanity to give Kate some room. "Clean towels are under the sink. Feel free to use anything in there you need."

"Thanks, Hunter."

I busy myself straightening my bedroom. Kate won't be spending any time in here, but just in case she gets a peek, she doesn't need to see dirty clothes all over the floor. If I don't want Kate, then why can I not stop thinking about the fact that she's naked in my shower?

Kate takes very little time in the bathroom. Kennedy is a total bathroom hog, so this is a nice surprise. I'm quick, too, but then I'm always quick. There's not much for a guy to do in the bathroom. Lather, rinse, dry off, shave, comb through my hair... done. Kate's in her bedroom with the door closed.

What is she doing in there? *Not my concern.*

I plop down onto the couch and power on the television. Maryland is playing Virginia. Perfect to get my mind off of Kate Richardson. It would be if she didn't choose this moment to pad into the room with her bare feet. She sits next to me on the couch, not too close, but close enough that her freshly-showered lavender scent engulfs me. She lifts her legs up and crosses them underneath her.

This is not going to work.

"Your claw-foot tub is amazing."

"I guess. It makes for a weird shower experience though."

"It's worth it for a bath, but then you probably don't take many of those." She smiles a soft smile that I return.

"No, can't say that I do."

This whole experience is completely surreal. Kate Richardson is here in my house. She's fresh from the shower, and she's sitting on my couch.

"Kate, I'm glad that you're staying for a while. It's nice to have a truce between us."

"The truce is nice, but using my mother to get me to stay was not cool."

Is she actually mad about that? The little smile that plays on her lips tells me *no*, but there's no telling with this woman. That was kind of low, but worth it because she's here.

"Have you heard anything from Brady?"

Her blue eyes are full of concern. Her hair seems

redder when it's damp, the waves cascading down her back. She's wearing a blue sweater and dark jeans that hug her legs, making my mouth water. I swallow heavily.

"No. Nothing. Listen, I know that you're probably tired, but is there anything that you'd like to do tonight?" *Because we have to get out of this house.* My fortifications are crashing around me.

She shrugs. "Oh, right. You have your plans tonight. I'm fine to stay here if you want to keep them."

"You could go with me."

I can't believe that those words came out of my mouth. I cringe. Kate will run back to Austin if she accepts my invitation.

"If you want me to." She looks unsure. "Are you sure it's okay if I tag along?"

"Oh, yeah. She'll be thrilled."

Kate's eyes widen. "Your date?"

Wait. What? "I'm not dating anyone. I'm talking about Granny. I usually take her to bingo on Saturday nights."

Kate's mouth morphs into a wide grin. "Sounds fun."

"Have you ever played bingo?"

"Nope."

"You're in for quite an experience. I just hope that you don't go back to giving me the evil eye after this. Just keep an open mind, or my selfishness for wanting to spend time with you might be my demise."

"You want to spend time with me?"

Shit. I shouldn't have said that out loud.

"I invited you to stay here, didn't I?" The words sound a little harsh, but Kate doesn't seem to notice. She smiles.

"You take your granny to bingo every week? You're a good grandson. A good brother, too."

This new Kate is difficult to understand. I knew what to do with her when she and her friends glared at me. I haven't seen her in person since that night in the closet—ten years ago—but I knew that wherever Kate was in the world, she hated me. She doesn't anymore.

"I have to warn you. Granny isn't...what's a nice way to say this? She isn't your typical *cookie-baking* grandma."

Chapter Seventeen

Kate

The house is cute. It is smaller than Hunter's, and where Hunter is minimalist with his decorating, his granny's home is the opposite. Every surface is covered with pictures and knickknacks. Framed family photos line the wall behind the television. Several of Hunter look back at me. His graduation photo is there. I know it well from many nights staring at it in my yearbook.

Hunter's granny is adorable. She has the family gray eyes, shoulder-length gray hair, and a happy, round face to go with her happy, round body. She isn't fat by any means, she simply has the curves that you would expect a grandma to have. She's wearing a dark green pantsuit with a button-down white blouse, and black boots. Am I underdressed? But, Hunter's wearing jeans, too—jeans that hug his body in amazing ways. *Down girl. Look his granny in the eye.*

"Beverly Simms, this is Kate Richardson."

Her whole face lights up as she gives Hunter a wide smile. Hunter doesn't return it. Why does he seem so nervous? I extend my hand toward her. Instead of shaking it, she takes it in her own and pulls me in for a hug.

"Please just call me Granny. Everyone else does."

"Thank you. It's nice to meet you."

"It's so nice to meet you, dear. Hunter has never brought a girlfriend to bingo before."

"Kate is a friend, Granny. We went to school together."

A pang of something shoots through my stomach. On one hand, I can't believe that Hunter called me his *friend*. That isn't a word we've ever used for each other. At the same time, I don't want to just be his friend. There's this electricity between us that he can't keep ignoring.

"Kate, do you have a boyfriend?"

"No, ma'am."

"Then you should be with my Hunter. He's a good man."

"Yes, ma'am. He is."

Hunter's eyes meet mine. He really is a good man. He shifts his feet uncomfortably and looks back at Granny.

"Let's get going. We still need to pick up Mildred, and if we don't move it, we're going to be late."

"Mildred isn't going this week. She's visiting her daughter and grandchildren in Richmond." Hunter's shoulders relax. "Byron Douglas is going instead."

Hunter stops walking. "Who?"

"Byron Douglas. I met him last week at the senior center. He lives in a nice house in town on Sycamore Street. All the girls have been trying to get their hooks in him, but tonight he's mine."

Granny laughs at her accomplishment. Hunter's eyebrows rise. A giggle escapes my throat. This is going to be interesting.

Bingo is at the fire station downtown. We arrive at the station with fifteen minutes to spare. The parking lot is pretty full, so we have to park three lanes over from the door. Hunter backs into the space just like everyone else has done.

"Bingo parking is like church parking. You have to be able to get out of here as quickly as possible."

Bingo is held in the room above the fire station. The elevator door opens to what at first appears to be chaos, but once my ears adjust to the noise level, I find that there's some organization to the craziness.

The bingo patrons sit at folding tables that are pushed together to form long rows. They chat away excitedly, while setting up their bingo cards and lucky knickknacks. Some people have little statues or pictures. Others go all out. One woman has a full assortment of little troll dolls arranged neatly on her table, sorted by their colorful hair in rainbow order.

Hunter ushers us to a table right in front of the bingo caller that is labeled with a *reserved* sign. He pulls out a seat for me.

"Wow, Officer Simms, the VIP table."

"I aim to impress."

A huge smile wraps around Hunter's face. He's freshly shaven, so I'm able to make out a tiny dimple on his left cheek. Why can't he always be this easy going around me?

He excuses himself to buy cards and daubers for us. Granny is all smiles at Byron, and he seems smitten with her as well. He's shorter than Granny, has a pretty big nose, very white hair, and two hearing aids. Granny acts like he's the stud of all studs. Byron seems dressed up for their date, too. He wears dress slacks and an oxford shirt, definitely a step up from what everyone else is wearing. They take their seats across from me. Hunter sits down and scoots his chair close to mine.

"If you're still speaking to me when this is over, it'll be a miracle."

He says it with a grin that just about takes my breath away. I swallow hard and smile back as Hunter begins explaining the rules and logistics.

Granny makes eye contact with me from across

the table. "I need to make a run to the concession stand. Kate, sweetie, will you come with me to help me carry?"

"Of course."

Granny stops to chat with several people on the way—a couple of them know my parents. Granny introduces me as Hunter's girlfriend. I don't correct her. When we finally arrive at the concession stand, she orders four cans of Coke and four cups of ice. I help her carry everything back to the table, where she passes them out to each of us.

"You know, I could really go for a chili dog. I wish I had thought of it when I was over there. Hunter, would you please get one for me? Kate, Byron, would you like one?"

Hunter tilts his head and gives Granny a funny look. It's just a chili dog. I'm not sure what the big deal is. He looks at me.

"I'd love one."

Hunter's brow furrows. "You like chili dogs?"

"I love chili dogs. With mustard and cheese, please, if they have it." *And onions, too, but hopefully onions are a bad choice for tonight.* A girl can dream.

Byron places an order as well, and Hunter disappears to fill it.

Once Hunter is across the room, Granny whips a stainless steel flask out of her purse that has the words *Keep on Truckin'* etched on the side. She immediately begins pouring liberal amounts of caramel-colored liquid into my cup, hers, and

Byron's. She's wearing a huge grin and doing this right out in the open. Shouldn't she at least be holding it under the table or something?

"Needed to get rid of him. Sometimes it isn't a good thing to have a policeman for a grandson. He doesn't like me to break the rules."

Hunter catches us giggling when he returns with our chili dogs.

"I don't even want to know."

We share another smile. "No, you don't."

The game begins. I do okay keeping up with my cards, but I only have six. Some of these people, including Granny, have them spread all across the table in front of them. Bingo is a lot more complex here than it was in school. First of all, a bingo isn't just a straight line or a cover all. There are other things you can have and still get a bingo—way complicated.

Where it was loud and talkative before bingo started, it's deathly quiet now. Only the sound of the caller and the balls popping in the machine can be heard. That is, until someone bingos, and then everyone has something to say.

"I only needed B-4."

"She won last week."

"You're calling the numbers too fast tonight."

"Bernie is a better caller."

"Where is he this week?"

This is fun for the people watching.

I take a swig of my drink to wash down the chili dog. *Wow!* The liquid burns as it travels down my throat to my stomach and then out to my extremities. I feel it everywhere. I'm not a big drinker, and Granny was pretty liberal with whatever that was—bourbon, maybe.

Hunter leans in and whispers in my ear. "You really do like chili dogs."

"Why wouldn't I?"

"I always pictured you eating gourmet food."

"Well, you were wrong. Now that I ate that, I have a hankering for Frito Chili Pie."

"I think I just fell in love."

Stop the presses. Did Hunter really just say that?

He looks away quickly while I down a huge gulp of my special drink.

Two more numbers are called before I'm with it enough to reengage in the bingo game. Hunter hasn't looked at me at all since he spoke those words. I fake bingo for the rest of the night, and I make chit-chat, but most of my brain power is concentrating on Hunter. He eventually looks at me. He happens to be watching me when Granny yells *bingo*. She startles me so much that I practically levitate off my chair.

It isn't even my bingo, but my palms are sweaty as Granny's numbers are called back to the caller to verify the game. This one is worth five hundred dollars. If I knew bingo could be this lucrative, I would have played before. The volunteer declares *a good bingo*, and she's presented with her winnings. A few people wish her well, but as I look around the room, I realize that most of the patrons have cleared out already.

"Since I won the big bucks, I'll treat for a late night snack. Hunter, drive us to Minnie's?"

"Sure, Granny."

We pile into Hunter's Jeep. Granny insists that she and Byron sit in the back, even though it's not easy for them to get in there.

Minnie's is a diner that's open almost all night long. It closes at two in the morning and then opens for breakfast at six. The restaurant has been around forever and is only a few blocks away. So, when we arrive, we have to help them both out of the back seat. Granny takes Byron's arm.

"It's so great that we're on a double-date."

Hunter looks at me, but this time, he doesn't argue with her. He shrugs and offers me his arm. I smile and take it. It feels good to hold onto him, even if it's just his arm. Just twenty-four hours and I've gone from *Why, God, does it have to be Hunter who saved me?* to *Thank you, God, for bringing Hunter back into my life.*

Hunter's sister, Kennedy, meets us at the door. Serving at Minnie's is her part-time job. She hugs Granny and Hunter, gives Byron and me big smiles, and walks us over to a booth near the back. Granny and Byron both order cocktails.

"Not for me, thanks. I'll take a club soda."

Hunter orders a coffee.

"No more bourbon and Coke for you?"

My eyes widen. "You knew?"

"Of course I knew. What kind of a police officer would I be if I didn't? I just pretend to be in the dark so that I don't have to do anything about it."

We giggle and look across the booth at Granny and Byron, who are both whispering to each other. Granny's cheeks are flushed, as is Byron's head. The blush of his head makes his white hair seem almost pink. What could they possibly be saying to each other? No, I definitely don't want to know. Suddenly this table feels like it isn't quite big enough for the four of us.

Luckily, we aren't at Minnie's for long. Granny and Byron say that they're tired and would like to go home. We say our goodbyes to Kennedy, heave our older companions into the Jeep, and Hunter begins the drive back to Byron's. It isn't far, but the trip feels like an eternity. I fiddle with the radio and exchange small talk with Hunter while we both try to ignore the strange noises coming from Granny and Byron in the backseat. *Awkward*.

"Byron asked me to come in for a night cap. Don't worry about me. He'll bring me home when we're finished."

Finished with what, I have no idea. I bite my bottom lip to stifle a laugh. Hunter doesn't look the slightest bit amused. Granny and Byron practically skip up his front walk. *Good for them.* They know what they want, and they aren't afraid to go for it. Maybe that's one of the benefits of old age.

Things aren't as cheery for me on the ride home. Hunter has clammed up. Totally silent. *What does this mean?* I make a couple comments about songs on the radio and the weather. Nothing from Hunter other than a literal grunt.

The situation doesn't improve when we get back to Hunter's house. The tension in the air is thick.

"You must be tired after the long day you've had. I'll see you in the morning." His tone is gruff, dismissive even. Just like that, he turns on his heel and walks away from me.

Really?

"You know what? Maybe it's better if I stay with my parents." He stops in his tracks. "Would you please drive me to their house?"

That gets his attention. Hunter turns and walks back toward me. His expression is unreadable, but the throbbing vein at the side of his temple tells me he's angry. Well, you know what? So am I.

"Why?"

"Geez, Hunter. You're like the king of mixed messages. One minute you embrace me like you're going off to war, and the next you act like you don't want to be anywhere near me. Would you make up your mind already?"

His lips descend on mine, hard and unyielding. My arms move around his neck to pull him closer. *Finally*. It's been so long since a kiss has left me this breathless and full of passion. Then I was afraid, but I'm not scared now. This feels...perfect.

Hunter pulls away and studies me, his eyes a startling emerald green. "How do you do this to me?"

The corners of my lips turn upward into a smile. "Me? You're the one who took so long to kiss me."

"Only because I don't want you to leave me again. Our last kiss was life-changing for me, and you didn't feel the same way."

It's as if all the air is sucked from the room.

"That kiss scared the crap out of me. I didn't know that it meant anything to you. Why didn't you tell me?"

He sighs heavily as his hands caress my neck, his touch sending electrical pulses down my spine.

"I tried to tell you that night, but you took off. I looked everywhere for you, and I went to your house the next day."

My face burns with the memory. I saw Hunter at the door, but I couldn't imagine what he wanted, and I was too nervous to face him. I never thought that he felt the same way.

"I was so afraid."

"Are you afraid now?"

"No." Years of longing and need bubble up inside

me—need that can only be quenched by Hunter.

Chapter Eighteen

Hunter

Kate looks up at me with those sky blue eyes. Her lips, swollen from my kisses, are parted slightly.

I'm done for.

There are no words.

I draw her to me as my lips move across Kate's slowly and deliberately. Our past kisses were unexpected, a crush of our lips together. This one is soft and how a first kiss should be—the beginning of the end for me. I push those thoughts out of my mind. This is Kate Richardson. The only girl I've ever really loved. Sure, she's going to leave me and break my heart, but she's here with me now, and I'm not going to waste one moment of the time we have together.

Her eyes flutter open bringing me back from my thoughts.

"Are you okay?"

Am I? Words still escape me. I reach down, slip my arm under her knees, and lift her up into my arms. A small squeak escapes from her throat when she realizes that I'm carrying her. A grin plays across my face. She returns it as her arms move around my neck. She isn't waif light, but she doesn't need to be. She's perfect, and she's here with me.

I carry her down the short hallway to my bedroom and lay her down gently on my bed. She studies me with uncertainty in her eyes.

It's my turn to ask. "Is this okay?"

Kate smiles a nervous smile. "Yes." The word comes out as a heady whisper that I feel in my gut.

I kick off my boots and lay down beside her. Her hand moves to my cheek. Her lips take mine. The touch of her tongue brings an explosion of feeling. Her hands travel down my chest and move under the hem of my t-shirt. She tugs upward. We break our kiss long enough to remove my shirt. Her hands move across my bare chest, her touch feather light as she explores. A moan escapes from somewhere deep inside me, and with it, a deep urge to move faster.

Slow down. If I'm going to have sex with Kate Richardson—and I sure hope that's what's happening here—I'm going to take my time. But that doesn't mean I have to go at a snail's pace. My fingertips find the hem of her sweater. There's a shirt underneath as well. I remove them both in one steady movement.

A light pink, lace bra, the color of Kate's now flushed skin reveals her perfect breasts. I suck in a breath.

"Beautiful."

She smiles as her skin turns an even darker shade of pink right before my eyes.

Kate's smile morphs to confusion and then panic. "Hunter? Are you here?" Brady's words cut into my hazy thoughts.

Shit. Brady's at the door.

Kate sits up quickly. I reach for her shirts and hand them to her. They're a jumbled mess since I pulled them off together. My shirt is not. I quickly pull it over my head, kiss Kate on the cheek, and head to the living room to head off Brady.

Great timing, buddy. I have no idea about how Brady would feel if I was with his sister. Would he be upset about that? Being with someone's sister is usually taboo, a line we don't cross. *Kate is different.* I knew her first. Years before Brady. That counts for something.

Brady rushes in as soon as I open the door. He hands me my toolbox.

"Thanks for letting me borrow this. I've been riding around with it all day, and the clanging sound it makes when I go over bumps is driving me crazy."

I set the toolbox down next to the door, lock up, and then find Brady in the kitchen with his head in my fridge.

"Were you able to stop the leak?" Seems like such a *normal* conversation to have under these strange circumstances.

"Yeah. It's not perfect, but it's not dripping water anymore."

I stop short of asking him if he wants me to take a look at it. Brady isn't handy, and although I could show him what to do, he doesn't like being reminded of his incompetency with tools. It's strange for him. He's definitely a manly kind of man in other ways, but he's somehow clueless in the ways of home improvements and car repairs. Previous attempts at these things have proved disastrous. He doesn't even own a wrench set, which is why he had to borrow my tools for a simple sink repair. It's just weird.

"That's great."

Brady looks up at my greeting. Dark circles line his shadowed eyes. His shoulders slump as he hands me a beer. I take it from his outstretched hand, and we plop down into the chairs surrounding my kitchen table.

"Where have you been?"

"I can't find her anywhere."

"You shouldn't have taken off. We can help you."

"I know, but I have to find her." The pleading in his voice is clear.

Brady nods his head in confirmation, props his

elbows on the table and then rests his head in his hands.

"Brady?" We both turn at the sound of Kate's voice. Her skin is still pink but probably not enough to be noticed by her brother. Her eyes are sharp as she studies him. She places her hand on his shoulder. Brady looks at her, but he doesn't stand to greet her. And now Kate's face is lined with worry, too.

I give Kate my seat next to Brady and get her a beer from the refrigerator. She folds her hands on the table and rubs her thumbs together. The urge to cover her hands with my own is huge, but I don't give in. She wouldn't want me to touch her right now.

"I looked for Jamie everywhere." Brady still stares straight ahead. "I even broke into her apartment."

"You broke into her home?"

"She lives on the second floor. I climbed up onto her balcony. Her sliding door was unlocked. I figure I had probable cause to enter. Jamie's missing."

"I can see that, but I don't want you messing up any evidence and getting in trouble with the FBI. They're investigating this now."

"Yeah. They showed up while I was there. The agents gave me some crap about being inside her place, but I answered their questions, and they let me go."

"Was it agents Cole and Rodriguez?"

"Yes. They mentioned that they were at the station earlier today."

"Did you find anything at Jamie's?"

"No. I don't think they did either, at least that I could tell. It looked like it always does. Her clothes were in her closet and her dresser. It didn't seem like she packed a bag or anything." *Always* isn't a word that Brady should use in this situation. He's only been seeing Jamie for a month, and she's been out of town for about half of that time.

"Where does she live?" I guess Kate has to be caught up on the particulars.

"Just outside of Charlottesville. She works up there and rents a small apartment on the west side of town."

"What's she like? I've seen a few photos on Facebook, but that doesn't tell me anything about her."

"She's smart, and she's beautiful. I told you that Jamie was special." Brady gives Kate a look that I don't quite understand, but some kind of communication passes between them. That much is clear.

Kate reaches her hand outward and places it on Brady's forearm. "I know you're smitten with Jamie, but you haven't known her very long. Sometimes you trust people too easily." Brady's brow creases. What Kate's saying is true, and it has to be said. I'm just glad that I'm not the one who said it. Brady's going to be pissed. Kate continues, "You do trust too easily, and you know it. It's not like this is the first time we've had this conversation. We need to look at Jamie objectively." Brady's body relaxes, but he still gives Kate a piercing stare. Kate's doing a great job of questioning her brother, so I just sit back and watch the dynamics between the two of them. "You've been dating Jamie for about a month, right?"

"Yeah."

"And during that time, how many trips has she made to Brazil?"

"Two trips. She goes to Sao Paulo every couple of weeks." Brady sighs heavily.

"Let's go over this again. She left on Sunday and came into town on Wednesday evening. Wouldn't she have arrived home in the morning? Did anything seem out of the ordinary?"

"Jamie seemed totally normal. She said that she arrives at different times depending on which flight she takes back. This time she was in a hurry to get back. She said she missed me and wanted to see me right away."

"Did she leave the bag with you intentionally? Maybe she knew she had some heat on her and..."

Brady cuts me off. "Jamie wouldn't do that."

"Knowing what we know about her already, she could do anything. She can't be trusted."

"Yes, she can. There has to be an explanation. Jamie couldn't be involved in this."

Kate lets out a sigh. Brady looks away, so she makes eye contact with me instead. *I'm with you.*

This is totally frustrating.

"What about you, Hunter? Did you get any weird vibes from her?"

"I never met her. We'd planned to meet twice, but she cancelled both times at the last minute."

"Apparently she didn't want to meet a policeman"

"It wasn't like that." Brady's forehead crease is back. "She had to work late. It happens."

"Did she have to work late often or just when she was supposed to meet me?"

His mouth opens to answer, but no words come out. A few beads of sweat break out on his forehead. His wheels are most definitely turning now. Poor guy. He means well, and he is a good guy. He really is too trusting. It's tough to see him suffer, but we have more questions that we need to have answered.

"Have you met Jamie's family or anyone else connected to her?"

"No, but it's only been a month."

"Do you know anything about her family? Where they live? Anything?"

"She told me that they live in Charlottesville. That's what I've been doing since I left her house earlier, trying to find them. I called everyone I could find in Charlottesville with the last name Adams, and that's a lot of people, but none of them claims to know Jamie." Brady sits up a little straighter in his chair. "Don't give me that look, Kate. They could have an unlisted phone number."

"Did our parents meet her?"

Brady fidgets in his chair. "No. She was supposed to come to Sunday lunch once, but something came up."

"Can you tell me more about Jamie's job?"

"Jamie's company is called Bio Fuel for Today. It's a non-profit that has some kind of government grant to study ethanol production. Her office is near Piedmont Community College. There may be an affiliation with the school, but I'm not one hundred percent sure."

"Why did she have to travel to Brazil?

"Sao Paulo is really good at creating ethanol from sugar cane. She works with a company down there to learn the technology and bring it here."

"What kind of degree do you need for that?"

Brady sighs and shakes his head. "I don't know. Maybe she told me, but I don't remember. She went to UVA. She grew up in Charlottesville."

"Did you ever meet anyone that she works with?"

"No. I did pick her up from work once. I just saw the parking lot, but I could tell the place was tiny. She spent about half her time there and the other half in Sao Paulo."

"She was bringing back diamonds from Brazil, right?"

Kate addresses her question to me more than to Brady, so I answer. "It looks that way."

"Jamie wouldn't do something like that. She's not that kind of person."

"You barely know her. She could have targeted

you all along and been using you as a patsy."

"That's impossible." Brady says the words without much gusto behind them. His whole body appears defeated. "We just need to find her coworkers or her family. I just pray that she's with them and not in danger herself."

Chapter Nineteen

Kate

I've been hard enough on Brady for tonight. He's a good person. It isn't his fault that he gives the world too much credit.

"You're right. I'm sure the FBI agents are working the family angle, too. They'll find them, and they'll find Jamie." I squeeze Brady's hand. "Why don't you get some sleep?"

"That sounds like a good idea," Hunter chimes in. "You can take Justin's room. It's just a twin bed, though. Is that okay?"

"Fine by me. Can I grab a shower?"

"Of course. Let me check things out back there. Be right back." Hunter stands and disappears down the hallway.

"I really am sorry about getting you involved in this."

"Stop saying that. Really. I'm glad that you're safe now, and I'm glad that I'm here to help you. We'll find Jamie." *Although when we do, I may punch her.*

Brady gives a completely unconfident nod.

"Although I should have told you, I'm not sorry about being friends with Hunter. You were wrong to hold a grudge for so long. He's a good guy."

My eyes moisten with tears. It's been a very long, emotional day.

"He is. You're right."

"You're all set, Brady. There are clean towels under the sink in the bathroom."

Brady stands. "Thanks, buddy." He slaps Hunter on the arm and heads down the hallway.

I take out my phone and do a quick search on Bio Fuel for Today. There's a company website, but it doesn't say much at all. There are no names of employees or photos or anything. There is a *contact us* button, but I don't dare contact them. They could all be involved in whatever diamond smuggling Jamie was doing. Were they, or was that just a side job for her?

Hunter takes a look at the website as well. "What do you think about all of this? Was Jamie using Brady?"

"It looks like it, but only she can answer that question."

I stand and stretch my arms over my head. What do we do now? We can't exactly go back to what we were doing before Brady showed up. That mood is totally gone.

"Come here." Hunter takes my hand and pulls me to him for a hug. His embrace is warm and comforting and just what I need right now.

"Brady's going to be okay."

"I know."

I pull back enough to look into Hunter's now light gray eyes.

"Do you think the bad guys have her? Jamie, I mean?"

"I sure hope not. I think she knew she was in trouble. That's why she gave Brady the bag in the first place. I figure she ditched her phone and took off after that." Makes sense.

I nod.

Hunter breaks our embrace and begins pulling me down the hallway. "Now, let's get you to bed. I hope you'll get some good rest." *I certainly wouldn't have gotten any rest with you tonight.* I know we're going to Kennedy's room, and we are. Hunter stops just outside the doorway. The sound of the running shower can be easily heard through the bathroom door just across the hall.

"I'm glad that you're back in my life, Hunter."

He kisses me lightly on the cheek. "Me, too. Goodnight, my Katie."

How am I supposed to sleep after that? Hunter called me *his Katie*. My heart melts again just remembering the way Hunter's voice sounded when he spoke those words. He's wonderful, and I'm an idiot for waiting so long to realize it.

If Brady hadn't gotten here when he did, I would be with Hunter right now. The thought leaves me disappointed. Big sigh. No one will even believe that we're together. I guess I should start with the person who will believe it the least—my friend, Melanie.

How do I even tell Melanie something like this? I'm too chicken to call her and say the words, even though she's surely still awake. Plus, I wouldn't want to wake up little Harry. That wouldn't be a good way to start this off. So, yeah, texting is the best choice for sure. Start with something simple.

I'm home for a few days. Until after Thanksgiving. Want to get together sometime this week?

I look at my screen and smile—lots of words and punctuation. I've never been one to take short-cuts with texting. People aren't lazy when they type an email. Why bother being lazy with this form of communication?

Yay! You're here. Can Harry and I come see you

tomorrow afternoon? I'd love to see your mom and dad.

Here goes nothing.

That won't work for Sunday. Long story, but I'm staying with Hunter Simms. Brady and I are here.

It might help to say that Brady's here, too. Maybe. I take in a deep breath and hit send. What does Melanie's expression look like right now? Is she staring at her screen in shock? Melanie was always my most supportive friend. She stood by me during the big *episode*, and she stood by me later when I should have been over it. I should have returned the favor when she needed me recently, but I wasn't here; I was in Austin. Sure, we had many late-night phone conversations where we studied her options and blasted the evil in her life, but I was too far away to be of any real use to her.

My phone vibrates, Melanie's photo displayed on the screen. With another deep breath, I answer.

"Hi."

"No way. Seriously?"

"Yes."

"How long have you been with him?"

"About twenty-four hours."

"Have you kissed him yet?" As usual, she gets

right to the point. I can't help but smile, whether it's about Mel's forwardness or Hunter's kiss. "You have! I want details."

I tell her everything.

Chapter Twenty

Hunter

Hues of pink and orange blanket the sky in anticipation of the sunrise. The sun winks at the sky before jumping to signal the new day. Winter is on the horizon for sure. We don't get sunrises like these in the warmer months. The temperature is in the thirties, another sign that winter is on its way.

I pull my Jeep into a spot next to the chief's pick-up. Minnie's isn't packed this early on a Sunday morning—that comes later after the church crowd —but, the regulars are here, and the chief is one of them. It feels like I was just here a few hours ago, and that's not far off.

I could hear Kate talking in her room last night.

Maybe it was Melanie or one of her friends from Texas who called, or maybe Kate needed someone to talk to and called someone. The murmurs made it difficult to fall asleep. Knowing Kate was just in the room next door and having just been reminded what she tastes like...it was a long time before sleep took me last night.

The chief's in his regular spot at the counter, an extra-large oval plate full of fried eggs, biscuits and gravy, sausage, and bacon before him. I snag the neighboring stool. His wife, Maybelle, is one helluva cook, but he's eaten his breakfast here nearly every day that I've known him. He says he's an early riser, and Maybelle is not, so he lets her sleep in. Normally, he's here just before work, so he's wearing his uniform. Not today. Today he's wearing overalls over a flannel shirt and work boots.

"Mornin', Simms."

"Sir."

Melinda, one of the waitresses, puts a cup of coffee on the bar in front of me. "What would you like this morning, Hunter?"

"Just coffee for now. Thanks."

She gives me a quick smile, refills the chief's coffee, and moves on to another patron.

"Figured I'd see you this morning."

"Why is that?"

His eyes study me over the rim of his coffee cup. "You've got a personal interest in this case. Am I right?"

Can't get anything past him. "You could say that."

"I've known Kate Richardson all her life. She's beautiful, smart, and a hard worker. Plus, I'd wager that she's a pretty fine cook to boot."

"I imagine she is." The chief's mouth takes on a small grin before he fills it with a bite of sausage. We need a change of subject. "Have you heard anything new about the case? Anything new about Jamie Adams?"

He chews slowly, as if buying himself time to form an answer.

"Unfortunately, we don't know anything new. We really need to find Ms. Adams. She would have some definite answers, but it looks like she's flown the coop. The FBI has checked out her apartment and found nothing useful. Jamie Adams appears to be her real identity. She's from Richmond. Both of her parents died in a car crash when she was younger. She has no close family. They're looking into some friends and associates but haven't found much. Or, if they have, they're not sharing the information. Rodriguez is usually pretty good about giving us what he has, so I would expect that if he had anything, he would run it past me."

"Any criminal history."

"Don't think so." He takes another thoughtful sip of coffee. "The three guys we nabbed yesterday aren't talking. Of course the FBI is checking them out as well."

I nod. "I hope we can find her and find her alive.

Obviously, she needs to pay for her crimes, but Brady needs some answers."

"Yes, he does."

Chapter Twenty-One

Kate

The clock reads 7:18 when I awaken, or should I say awaken again? It was a fitful night of sleep. My dreams vacillated back and forth between visions of being held at gunpoint and tied to a chair to visions of Hunter's bare chest. Although I obviously prefer naked thoughts of Hunter, neither allowed for a restful night.

If the level of brightness is any indication, it's going to be a warm day. Of course, it's usually still dark when I awaken at home. I'm generally a morning person. I can't help it that I get up so early, but I've learned to take advantage of it. Morning is by far my most creative time of the day, when some of my best blog and design ideas pop into my head. But, I don't usually stay awake until two in the morning talking on the phone with my friends and thinking too much.

I stretch and take a look at my surroundings. It isn't just Kennedy's walls that are pink. Pink can also be found in her bedspread. It does match. It's just that this particular shade leaves me feeling like I'm on the inside of a Pepto Bismol bottle. After another stretch, I get up out of bed. I open the door and listen. Nothing. So I take care of my bathroom business and shuffle to the kitchen in search of coffee.

Notes from both Brady and Hunter are on the table. Hunter's note states that he's gone to town, and he'll be back soon. Brady's simply says that he'll see us soon. My heart squeezes for him. I know that he likes Jamie—he told me about her right after he met her—but hopefully he hasn't fallen too hard. He wants to find her, and I get that, but she's some kind of criminal. He can't still be interested in her after all of this. Maybe he needs answers not just about the case, but also about how he fit into her life.

A click or a clank or some kind of noise comes from the back of the house. I just about jump out of my skin.

What the heck was that?

The answer comes quickly as the air begins blowing through the heating vent. The enormous relief puts a nervous smile on my face. I live alone at home, and I've never been a jumpy person. I guess all of that goes out the window now that I've almost died twice this weekend, Even more than that, I'm in a strange house. *Get it together.*

With a huge sigh, I head towards the coffee pot, thrilled to find a warm pot waiting for me. A little bowl of sugar and a spoon are on the counter as well. Hunter is so thoughtful. How could I have spent years hating him? I do remember why, but that time seems like such a waste. This morning would have been decidedly different if Brady hadn't shown up last night when he did.

Me and Hunter Simms. *Unbelievable.*

I take my coffee and my phone to the couch. I wrap the quilt around me to ward off the early morning chill. In my business of home decorating, I've run across many quilts. I've never made one myself, but I can recognize that this one is spectacular. It's composed of an intricate pattern in greens and grays—like Hunter's eyes—and the entire thing is hand-stitched. And it's soft and warm, which is the point of a quilt in the first place.

I busy myself with checking email and my blog. There are several comments and a few questions about Friday's *Regifting with Flair* post. Who would have thought that I would have had so much to say after cleaning out my bathroom linen closet? It's amazing and ridiculous how much junk people can hold onto just because they feel obligated to keep it. Did I really need eight types of bubble bath? How about four loofas? No one needs that many, but they were included in gift baskets that I received, so I kept them. I will *never* use them, so I wrapped them up in some empty baskets that I had and gave them to two of my elderly neighbors whom I happen to know love bubble baths.

My thoughts drift to the clawfoot tub just down the hall. If I had a tub like that, I might be more willing to take a bath. Especially if Hunter was with me.

Yikes, I have it bad.

Speak of the devil, Hunter picks this moment to walk inside. The telltale prickle of embarrassment crawls up my neck to my cheeks. *Geez. Get a grip.* Hunter doesn't know I was just thinking about him in the bathtub. Besides, he'd probably like to know that's how I was thinking of him.

"Hey." It isn't just the one-word greeting that swirls my insides. It's Hunter's smile as well. A crooked kind of grin that makes it seem like he knows a secret.

Could he tell that I was picturing him naked? My face feels even hotter. Time to deflect.

"You were out early. Everything okay?"

Hunter removes his jacket and hangs it on a hook next to the front door. The collar of a plaid cotton shirt peeks through the rim of a dark green sweater. The shade of green goes perfectly with his now light green eyes. He kicks off his boots and steps towards me.

"I met the chief at Minnie's for coffee. He's there early every morning, and I wanted to get the scoop on the case."

"What did you learn?"

"Why don't you sit with me in here?" He gestures towards the kitchen. "I know we're going to your parent's house for lunch, but right now, I'm starving."

"Me, too."

I fold the quilt and place it carefully on the end of the couch. "This quilt is beautiful. Who made it?"

"My mom. She made one for each of us kids. That's one of the few things that we have from her that really matters."

"Oh, I'm sorry. It was just lying here. If I'd known that, I wouldn't have used it."

"Don't be sorry. It's okay to use it. That's why it's there. She would hate it if the quilt was never used." *Phew.*

I stand and follow Hunter to the kitchen. He opens a cabinet and takes out two bowls.

"Will you grab the milk? I hope you like cereal. That's all that I have for breakfast."

"Sure. Cereal's great." I place the milk jug on the counter next to the bowls and now spoons that Hunter has added.

"Hopefully, there's something here you will like."

Is this another thing about gourmet food or some other such nonsense? Before I can say a word, I catch a glimpse of Hunter's cereal collection.

Collection is definitely the right word. One entire cabinet is filled with cereal, and not just any cereal either. It's as if Hunter walked down the cereal aisle and put one box of every kind of sugary-sweet, cavity-forming flake into his cart. No fiber or raisins here. Only bright colors and marshmallows.

"Wow. This is incredible." He smiles shyly. "Is this what you eat for breakfast every morning?"

"Pretty much," Hunter replies as he pours himself a healthy portion of Fruity Pebbles. "This is my one indulgence."

"What do you mean?"

"Well, when I was young, my mom would only let us have this kind of cereal as a rare treat, too unhealthy and all that. Then...um *after*...we couldn't afford it. Now that I can afford it, I think I'm making up for lost time." Hunter smiles, but it's shy and unsure.

I flash him a huge smile. "This is great." His shoulders visibly relax. "I haven't had Lucky Charms in forever. My mom was the same way." I pour a heaping portion of the colorful cereal into my bowl and add as much milk as the bowl will take without causing the cereal to spill over the sides.

We sit down together at the kitchen table and chow down. The taste of the sugary sweetness brings back memories of snow days and homework. It's funny how memories are attached to certain scents and tastes. Songs can also bring a rush of memories and feelings. I haven't listened to *In Your*

Eyes by Peter Gabriel for what, sixteen years now—not since the incident with Hunter. Mom loved that song and played the CD a lot until I would freak out or leave the room whenever it came on. That song always made me think about Hunter and his beautiful green eyes. After everything that happened, I couldn't listen to it anymore. Now that we're friendly again, do I get to have that song back?

"What are you thinking about?"

"What?" Hunter's eyes study me, his face set.

"You were deep in thought just now. Care to share?"

Not really. "Just everything that we're going through, I guess. What did you learn from Chief Tisdale?"

Hunter stirs his spoon around the milk in his bowl, pushing his remaining colorful Fruity Pebble flakes around. Is he avoiding the question or just thinking of how to form his answer? Wait. Why does he need to think about his answer? My body straightens in my chair. Hunter's eyes dart to me.

"Sorry. I really don't know anything new. It's just...I know that Brady likes Jamie, and I understand how he wants her to be innocent." Hunter lets out a big sigh. "I just don't see any way for her to be innocent."

A sigh escapes me as well. Hunter's right, and when the truth comes out, Brady is going to be devastated. Hunter's worry over Brady is yet another testament to what a great guy he is. I let one mistake—from elementary school no less—be an excuse to hate Hunter for too many years. Hunter's a warm and caring person. *Warm.* After the bit we shared last night, how can my thoughts not go there?

As if reading my mind, Hunter's eyes darken to a deep emerald. I reach my hand across the table, and he takes it. His fingers intertwine with mine. I pull him to a standing position and place my free hand against his chest.

"Oh, Katie. There's no denying I want you, but I don't want to rush anything."

"I think we've waited long enough."

I turn and walk down the hallway to Hunter's bedroom, pulling him with me. This forwardness isn't like me. At all. But I don't feel the least bit shy. I want Hunter, and I don't want to wait another minute.

He turns me to face him, and I place my hands on his shoulders. Hunter's hands move to my chin, cupping it gently and tilting my head upward as his lips move to mine. They brush together slowly, the contact buzzing between us. My lips part, and our kiss deepens. Hunter takes his time, exploring my mouth fully. I explore him, too, with my tongue and my hands as they travel over his body.

He pulls away slowly, his eyes locked with mine. They're an even deeper green now and so full of emotion and the same need that I know is reflected in my own. He places one hand on my shoulder while his other gently caresses my cheek.

Suddenly, it feels as if Hunter has on way too many clothes. I work the sweater over his head and then free each button of his shirt only to find a white t-shirt underneath. My gaze leaves Hunter's only long enough to unwrap each layer until I reach his bare chest. I break eye contact to take peek. *Wow!* His chest is tight and muscular, and the V on his abdomen practically points to what will be revealed next. A whimper escapes from my throat as my fingers jump to explore. Hunter's lips curve up into a smile that I return.

Do not fall apart here. Just enjoy.

My eyes lock again with Hunter's, broken only when he lifts my pajama shirt over my head. The swoosh of his breath travels across my skin. No bra for me this morning, and Hunter's look of awe tells me that he appreciates that. He cups my bare breast as a moan escapes from deep in my throat.

What is up with all these noises I'm making? My body has never made involuntary sounds during sex.

"You're amazing, Katie."

My chest tightens. Hunter's amazing, too. In so many ways. Why didn't I see that sooner?

My fingers move to the fly of his jeans. I tug them down until Hunter kicks them off. He removes his socks one by one. A pair of navy blue boxers are all that remains on his body. I know that only from what I see in my peripheral vision. His eyes still have me mesmerized.

Hunter tugs on the elastic waistband of my pajama bottoms, and they fall to my feet. I step out of them and crawl onto the bed. Hunter removes his boxers and lies down next to me. He traces my jawline and then my lips before taking them with his own. His kiss is soft and slow. Warmth spreads through me, gentle at first, but then hotter and hotter as our kisses intensify. My hands move over his body in a desperate attempt to take it all in.

Hunter's kisses move to my neck and then my shoulder. He lifts his head to study my breasts. My skin warms.

"I love it when you blush like that."

That just makes me blush even more. Hunter smiles and then kisses my breast. He explores each one fully. My hands move through his hair. My body is on fire. He lifts his head and turns his attention to my panties. He slowly traces the lines of them with his finger and then brushes over my middle. My body arches toward Hunter's. His lips curve upwards to form that wicked smile he does so well. Hunter's enjoying this. I am, too, but I can't wait any longer. The need pulsing through my body is more than I've ever known.

I reach down and remove my panties myself. Hunter moves on top of me. The weight of him and the touch of his skin against mine is almost more than I can handle. His eyes are there again, locked with mine as our bodies become locked together as well. Hunter moves again, slowly as if this one movement is going to take both of us over the edge, and it might. I'm so close.

Again I cry out. The intensity of being one with Hunter claims my whole being.

He begins his rhythm, and in practically seconds, we're both over the edge, holding each other tightly. He says my name in a moan as we plummet together. My body explodes in a vortex of swirling energy and bursting colors.

Chapter Twenty-Two

Hunter

Kate clings to me as our breathing returns to normal. Her entire body, not just her face and neck, is flushed from our lovemaking. Does her whole body always turn this color when she blushes? Just that thought, and I'm already beginning to harden again.

That was way too fast. What does she think of me?

"Kate?"

She smiles. Oh gosh. *Kate Richardson is here in my bed.*

"I don't know what happened. Suddenly it was just too much. My body just wouldn't wait. It was..."

What can I say? I don't have words to describe what that was. It wasn't just a physical act. It was more like our souls came together in perfect harmony. What the hell? One time with Kate, and she has me thinking about my soul.

Kate's smile widens, her entire face brightens.

"I couldn't wait either." She averts her eyes shyly for a few seconds before making eye contact again. "You have nothing to apologize for. That was the most intense experience of my entire life."

She means those words, too. Her eyes widen slightly, and her lips part as if she just surprised herself by telling me something so personal. My eyes are focused on her lips now. I claim them again. One good thing about being quick is that we have lots more time to do it again.

There are still no words. Kate's head rests in the crook of my arm as she sleeps peacefully. We both nodded off for a while, but now I lay awake just watching her. Her skin has returned to its normal porcelain color. She has five light freckles on the bridge of her nose and more on her cheeks. *Shit*. This is bad, worse than I could have ever imagined. I've always known that I liked Kate, even when I've tried to ignore it. She doesn't even live here. She has a life in Austin that doesn't include me. She's happy there, too. I hear things. A small part of me looked forward to her time at school ending, so that she would come home. She never did. She was dating some guy named Clint then, and she stayed in Austin. I didn't know her family then, but this is a small town and word gets around. Kate dated him for four years, and there was even some talk of marriage. When I heard that they broke up, I was more excited than I wanted to admit. I thought she'd surely move home then. She didn't. All this tells me that she's happy in Austin. She's made a life for herself there.

Why would she choose to stay here in Davidson with all that Austin has to offer? My brother, Justin, talks about Austin like it's the best place he's ever been. He goes there pretty often; it's a short drive from where he's stationed in San Antonio.

Enough of this. Kate is here with me now, and I'm going to make the most of every minute I have with her. I'm going to be with her and *be with her* every chance I get. Do not think about how the best moments of your life will be the ruin of it.

Kate stirs, and her eyes flutter open.

"That wasn't a dream?" She leans up on her elbow and grazes my cheek with her soft lips. I push all those thoughts out of my head, which is not hard to do with Kate smiling at me like she is. Her smile is somehow knowing and shy at the same time. How does she pull that off?

"If it's a dream, then I haven't woken up yet either, and I don't ever want to." A tinge of pink touches her cheeks. I lightly kiss her cheek, feeling the warmth of it on my lips. "My Katie."

She smiles the most amazing smile and then sighs. "We're due at my parents' house in an hour."

That's true. I'd been watching the clock as I watched Kate sleep, not sure when to wake her up, but not wanting to give up on this time together either.

"Would you like the shower first?"

"Yes, please."

Kate plants a quick kiss on my lips and then rolls out of bed. She reaches down and takes her clothes with her, but she doesn't get dressed, cover herself with a sheet, or make any fuss about being naked in front of me. That's the biggest turn on so far. She smiles one more time before heading out the door.

The house is too quiet. I'm dressed now and ready to go, and Kate is nowhere in sight. I thought she was in the living room, but she's not here. A knot forms in the pit of my stomach as I rush to Kennedy's room. She's not there either.

Stay calm. She has to be around here somewhere. "Kate?"

No answer.

The knot begins to churn and grow. A vision of Kate tied to that chair flashes through my mind. Where is she?

"Kate!" Still nothing.

I rush to the front door and throw it open. "Kate!" I strain my ears. Nothing.

The churning has given way to full-on panic. I run off the porch and around the house, screaming her name again.

She's there. She stands at the back of the house looking down at the creek. Her back is to me. The churning and sloshing of my stomach stops suddenly, leaving a wave of dizziness in its wake. Kate turns toward me as I place my hands on my knees for support. This is too much.

"Hunter, are you okay?" She's here now, standing next to me, her eyes set with worry.

"What are you doing out here?"

Realization dawns on her face, but there's a fire in her eyes. "I was just looking around. It's really pretty back here, and I found some really cool rocks by the creek."

No longer lightheaded, I stand to face her. "You could have told me." The words come out a bit harsh, but they need to be said.

"You were in the shower. I didn't want to bother you, and I didn't realize that I had to check in with you for permission just to stand in your yard." She stands just a bit straighter.

Shit. This isn't what I want. I want Kate warm and soft and in my bed. I don't want to go back to the fighting. A heavy sigh escapes from deep inside me.

"I'm sorry that I overreacted. I couldn't find you,

and I was worried. I couldn't stop thinking about what happened yesterday, and I freaked out."

Her expression softens. "I'm sorry, too. I didn't think that I was in danger, even after what happened yesterday. I feel safe here with you, and besides, I'm not exceptionally good at being told what to do."

She steps toward me, and my arms move around her to pull her even closer. The scent of lavender fills my nose. It reminds me of the hug we shared yesterday when we left the cabin, but so much has changed since then. Yesterday, I wouldn't let myself feel this way. I wouldn't let myself breathe in her scent and everything about her. I've given in. I take another deep breath and then another, hoping to imprint this moment on my brain forever.

Chapter Twenty-Three

Kate

"Right on time," Hunter states with a smile as he pulls into my parents' long driveway. He's trying to appear at ease, but his eyes betray him. He's nervous. Why? He seems chummy with my family. Is it because we're now an item? "Brady's here, too. I wondered if he would be." Sure enough. Brady's car is parked next to a black Honda Civic that I don't recognize.

It took less than ten minutes to get here, but those ten minutes were pretty silent. Nothing about the silence felt awkward. We're both still processing what happened between us this morning, and there's a lot to process. It isn't just that Hunter and I did the deed, it's the deed itself. Before this morning, I'd only ever had sex with two men.

My first was Warren. We dated from freshman into the fall of sophomore year of college. He was a good guy. We just weren't going in the same direction. Then there was Clint. Clint was a lot more complicated. We met when we were seniors and dated for four years. Clint was good looking and smart. I thought at the time that I loved him. It was the sex that finally got me really thinking about things. The sex with Clint and Warren was pleasant. It was maybe a little more than that...enjoyable? That's not the right word exactly either, but it was most definitely not the mind-blowing, epic experience I just shared with Hunter.

"Sit tight. I'll get your door." Wow. A man with manners. My father drilled that kind of thing into Brady's head, one of the few men that I've seen do that.

I give Hunter my hand and allow him to pull me up. I help as much as I can though because lifting this body can't be easy. I'm not exactly model thin. Of course, Hunter's already seen me naked, so he knows all about that. Did it just get warmer out here?

I give Hunter a quick kiss and take his hand. Our fingers intertwine naturally. "I wasn't sure you'd want them to know."

"I want everyone to know." The smile on Hunter's face warms me even more.

"That's good because your mom is watching us from the window."

Mom opens the door for us with a squeal of delight. "I always wondered about you two."

"What are you talking about?" Brady rounds the corner from the living room and zeros in on our clasped hands. His small smile morphs to a bitter scowl. Hunter doesn't let go of my hand, but he does stand a bit straighter. "What the hell, man?"

I release Hunter's hand, step forward, and place my hands on Brady's chest. "I knew Hunter long before you did, so don't even play the friends don't sleep with friends' sisters card."

Crap. I can't believe I just said that.

"You slept with her?"

Hunter's eyes widen into huge circles. *Oops.* I want the world to know I like Hunter, not that I'm sleeping with him. Brady sticks out his chest. *No! The last thing we need is some kind of fight.* Brady lets out a deep breath, and his chest falls back to normal. His shoulders slump.

Brady's eyes meet mine. "I guess I just never saw this coming. I thought you hated him." He gestures toward Hunter. "Mom's been a nervous wreck worrying about how you'd react when Hunter and his family come here for Thanksgiving next week."

"What are you talking about?"

Mom plasters a very nervous smile on her face and steps toward me. "I was a bit worried about you being upset, but everything has turned out great." If it's so *great*, then why is Mom wringing her hands together?

A movement in the family room catches my eye. Kennedy is sitting on the couch, watching us intently.

Hunter's sister is here for Sunday lunch.

"How long have they been coming here?"

"Since sometime over the summer. Hunter came a couple times by himself, and once I learned about Kennedy, I insisted that she come over, too."

That's just like Mom, making sure everyone is taken care of. I fold my arms in front of me and see that Brady is in almost the same stance. We really are a lot alike.

"They weren't here when I came home in August."

"No, they both knew that you were visiting then, and they declined my invitation those two weekends. They both gave excuses that they had other things to do, but I know they were fibbing. I wouldn't let them get out of Thanksgiving dinner. Their Granny's coming, too. "

I sneak a peek at Hunter. He looks cautious, like I might blow any second. He's right. I might. Brady kept their friendship a secret for more than a year. Hunter's been hanging out with my parents, too. As far as my family knows, I hate Hunter. They became friends with him anyway. Those thoughts pass through my mind a few times but don't get the response I would expect. So, why am I still mad? The realization hits me hard. *My family knew how great Hunter is, and they didn't tell me.* My cheeks warm up yet again, but this time it isn't with anger so much as the realization that Hunter could have been in my life sooner.

Is it just a simple matter of timing? Nothing about my relationship with Hunter has ever been simple. I've had plenty of chances to make things right between us. Hunter came to see me here in this very house the morning after we kissed in that closet, and I made Mom send him away. I was too chicken to face him then.

I wasn't scared when Hunter gave me that apology note for standing me up. Then I was stubborn and stupid. Still, I saved the note. It's upstairs in my old bedroom in my jewelry box. Something made me keep it—probably the same something that made me think of Hunter more often than I should have. I'd come to the conclusion that we weren't meant to be. Fate was against us—at least I always thought so. But it was fate that made me go to the cabin on Friday night. It was fate that Hunter was the one to find me there. Maybe fate's been pushing us together all this time. I can't just go around deciding what my fate will be. Fate does that for me.

"Are you angry?"

Mom's words break me out of my trance. She

stands in front of me fisting her apron nervously. I pull her to me in a tight hug.

"Honestly, I'm a little mad." Mom takes in a quick breath. "You guys all got to have more time with Hunter than I have. That doesn't seem fair."

A collective whoosh of relief seems to come from everyone in the room. I reach my hand out to Hunter. He takes it and then pulls me into a tight embrace. My cheek presses warmly into his chest. "I guess this is about as good as this situation could have gone down." I lean back and see Hunter's smile. It warms me completely. I place a kiss on his cheek and turn to Brady.

Brady looks more confused than ever. I need to be careful in front of him, at least until he gets used to the idea of Hunter and me as a couple. I've never really been physical with any man in front of him. Brothers are protective of their sisters, and Brady is no exception. Well, except for the fact that he was hanging out with my sort-of enemy behind my back, but I'm going to let him slide on that right now. He hugs me, and then I hug Mom again. When I pull away from her, Kennedy is here with us, too, so I hug her as well. Kennedy's eyes are wet with tears. I realize that mine are as well. Why not? This is too much.

"Where's Dad?"

"He's out back manning the grill." Lucky Dad. He will be thrilled that he missed this display of feminine emotion.

"Let's go see if he needs any help," Hunter says with a look at Brady. They disappear into the kitchen.

Chapter Twenty-Four

Hunter

That went a hell of a lot better than expected. The deception had to come out at some point. I've been coming over here for lunch almost every Sunday since the beginning of June. Kate's family just sort of took me in. Grace invited me over right after the robbery, but I wouldn't accept. She wouldn't take *no* for an answer and finally wore me down. We had a nice lunch even if it was a little awkward from time to time whenever Kate's name came up in conversation.

I embraced everything about it, since I hadn't had a family meal like that in too many years to count. Brady invited me fishing not long after that, and then, eventually, I was included in Sunday lunch every weekend. Grace was insistent that I be here for Thanksgiving dinner this year, even though she knew that it might upset Kate.

"It's time to pull off the Band-Aid," she'd said only two weeks ago. "What happened between you and Kate was so long ago. Kate can't still be holding a grudge for what happened between you two." Did she mean the original incident all the way back in the sixth grade or the more recent kiss? It's been ten years since that kiss, but sometimes it still feels very fresh. Well, felt fresh. It's definitely fresh now, considering our morning together.

We find Albert standing next to a grill full of bratwurst. He waves at us with the large tongs in his right hand. He's smiling and completely oblivious to the scene that just played out inside the house.

"Hope y'all are hungry."

"I'm starving."

"I bet you are," Brady retorts, giving me the evil eye. Good mood gone. I've given that look to enough of Kennedy's boyfriends to know what's going on inside Brady's head.

"Look, I know you're upset about me being with your sister, but I really care about her." Brady's expression remains impassive. He crosses his arms over his chest again. "I've had a crush on Kate since the second grade." He tilts his head. His eyes roll as if to say *Is that the best you can do?* "It's true. We drove each other crazy all through school. Besides, I wouldn't be with her now if we hadn't ended up in the cabin together on Friday night."

"What happened in the cabin?"

"Absolutely nothing happened in the cabin. Luckily, I was there to save her. I built a fire. That was it. The point is that Kate and I have been fighting this *whatever this is* for a long time. Fate brought us together that night, and what happens, happens. This is not a fling. I care about Kate a lot, and I always have. Give me a chance."

Brady sighs heavily. His arms fall to his sides. "You know I like you, but Kate's my sister. Do not fuck this up."

"I won't."

"Fine."

Brady sure doesn't look fine. He looks like shit. His shiner is a little better, but the deep, dark circles under each eye are seemingly even darker against his pale skin.

"Did you get any sleep?"

"Not really."

Albert chooses this time to interrupt. "Brady, I forgot a platter. Would you please go inside and get one?"

"Sure, Dad." Brady takes off for the house.

"Listen Hunter. Kate has always had feelings for you." *What?* Albert shrugs his shoulders. His blue eyes, the same as Kate's, seem to laugh at my shocked expression. "She put a little too much energy into hating you. Brady might not realize that, but I do. I'm not as in the dark about these things as everyone around here would like to believe. I know that you care about Kate, and I know you'll treat her right."

"Yes, sir."

"But that doesn't change the fact that I'm Kate's father, so like Brady said, don't fuck it up."

Chapter Twenty-Five

Kate

"Sorry you had to witness my meltdown, Kennedy."

The two of us are left alone together in the kitchen when Mom and Brady go into the dining room to find a platter. The poor girl has learned a lot about me in the last few minutes—at the very least, that I'm sleeping with her brother. Her long, chestnut hair is back in a ponytail again. She looks back at me with her gorgeous green eyes—green eyes that apparently stay green all the time—and smiles.

"No worries here. Brothers can be a real pain in the butt when it comes to dating."

"It wasn't just that, though. It started because I

had a hissy fit about my family having Hunter over all this time and not telling me. Hunter and I...well, we haven't always gotten along very well." *That's an understatement.*

"Things seem to be working out now." Her lips curve into a gorgeous smile, revealing perfect, white teeth. This girl is beautiful. I bet Hunter has quite a time keeping the guys away from her.

"Yeah, I guess they are." I can't help but return her smile with one of my own.

Brady stands in the doorway. He is not smiling. Actually, he looks terrible. It's as if his entire body slumps with exhaustion. I wish there was something that I could do to help him. I step forward and give him a tight embrace. It really ticks me off that this Jamie woman involved Brady in her mess. She's probably on a beach somewhere while my brother is sick with worry and being questioned by the FBI.

"I have to get this out to Dad." I let go and watch him walk outside.

"Mom, what do you think about Jamie?"

"Never met her. I asked Brady to invite her over to Sunday lunch a couple times, but she was either out of town or had other plans."

"Yeah. That's the excuse she seemed to give everyone. Either she is a very busy person, or she was avoiding everyone that Brady wanted her to meet."

❖❖❖

My mouth waters as I survey the spread before us. There's bratwurst, cheesy potatoes, green beans, and black-eyed peas. Winston, my parent's cocker spaniel, is lying under the table in front of me, her head resting on my shoe. Her eyes are trained on me as she waits patiently for bites of food to be dropped her way. This is what home is all about. There are so many memories that I've made here at this very table, eating delicious food and talking over the events of the day. It feels even better with Hunter next to me. Kennedy and Brady are across from us. Kennedy flashes me another bright smile. I've missed being home.

One good thing about my family entertaining Hunter behind my back is that I don't have to be embarrassed by Mom's dishes. Mom's preoccupation with Elvis is borderline creepy. That's okay right now because Hunter already knows. On Sundays, she pulls out her "good china." Much to the embarrassment of her children, Mom's "good china" is a special edition commemorative set with a different Elvis depiction on each plate. I currently have *Jailhouse Rock* Elvis. Hunter has what I've always called *Army Elvis*, which is Elvis wearing his army uniform and smiling proudly. I scoop up some potatoes and plop them down on Elvis's face. There, that's better. I'm not freaked out by it as an adult, but when I was younger, it seemed like Elvis was always staring at me while I was trying to eat. My plates at home are solid colors—so much easier to eat off of them.

"Are you really able to stay here until after Thanksgiving?" Mom asked the question, but everyone except for Hunter is staring at me awaiting my answer. Hunter's gaze is fixed on his black-eyed peas, which he is moving around with his fork.

"I'm planning on it." *I don't feel the urge to run back to Austin anymore, and I'm not sure how that makes me feel.* I've made a good life for myself there. "I have a few things that I was supposed to do at home this week, but they're nothing that I can't postpone."

Hunter's shoulders relax. Mom looks from me to Hunter, sighs, and then smiles a huge smile of relief. Dad smiles, too.

Dad clears his throat. "Will you be staying with Hunter for your entire visit, or will we get to have you here for some of the time?"

Um.

"Honestly, just having you in the same state makes me happy." The room feels a bit lighter when Dad smiles. I'm a grown woman and all, but having this conversation with my father is still unnerving.

"We'll have to see how the investigation progresses, but until we're sure that Kate is completely out of danger, she'll be safer at my house."

Brady opens his mouth as if he's about to argue but closes it before speaking. *Thank goodness.* We don't need any more trouble between the two of them. Kennedy doesn't speak, but her huge smile is enough. Once we make eye contact, she ducks her head and stares at her food. Her smile doesn't fade though.

The ring of Hunter's phone cuts through the temporary silence. He excuses himself as he answers the call and walks into the living room. Our lunch conversation doesn't resume. We strain to hear what we can from Hunter's side of the call, which isn't much. That's what I'm doing anyway, and I figure everyone else is, too, because no one says anything except for Hunter. He says only a few words before returning to the table. He doesn't take his seat.

"That was the Chief. They're going to begin a search for Jamie. Her car was found on a dirt road behind the Franklin property, so we're going to search the area."

"I'm coming with you." Brady stands. Of course he wants to go.

"I can help, too."

Hunter frowns. "I don't think that's a good idea. They haven't opened the search up to volunteers yet, and I can't show up with both of you."

"But..."

"Come here."

Hunter grabs my hand and pulls me into the living room. He stands close to me. His hands rest on my shoulders as if he literally wants me to stay put.

"I'd really like it better if you stayed here with your parents and Kennedy. Maybe Kennedy can give you a ride back to my place later. Will you please do this for me?"

"I can help. The more eyes looking for Jamie, the better."

"I have a really bad feeling about this. It's not going to turn out well." Hunter tenderly brushes my cheek with his knuckles. "You've been through enough."

"I'm not a baby, Hunter. I can handle it."

"I can't."

My heart swells, and my stomach tightens. He leans in slowly and brushes his lips lightly against mine. His touch brings a warmth to my entire body. *He cares about me.*

I pull back enough to look Hunter in the eyes. "I know that you're only doing this to distract me."

"That's not the only reason."

"I'm going to give you some slack here. It's nice that you're taking Brady with you, so I'll back off. You have to promise to call me if you learn anything at all. If you find a clue or if you find her." *Alive though, please somehow find her alive.*

"I will. I promise."

Hunter gives me one more peck on the cheek and heads back to the dining room. I follow him in a daze. My lack of sleep and morning of lovemaking are catching up with me. It's not like I had a restful night of sleep the night before when we were in the cabin either.

"Kennedy, do you mind taking Kate home later? I

mean…to our home?" Hunter blushes and flashes a nervous smile.

Kennedy smiles, too. "Of course not. It'll give us time to hang out."

"Thank you for the great meal, Albert and Grace."

"I wish you could have eaten a bit more before you had to go. We'll save some for you. You boys be careful out there."

"Yes, ma'am. Ready Brady?"

Brady stands, kisses Mom on the cheek, and walks toward the front of the house. Hunter gives me one last tentative smile before he leaves as well.

The rest of our lunch is subdued. There's definitely good conversation, but it's obvious that our minds are on Hunter and Brady. Mine sure is. There's plenty to worry about with Brady, but for me, it's more than that. There is a definite void without Hunter here. That's something that I can't allow myself to think about right now. It's too new and too scary. I'm still getting used to the idea that I like Hunter. I'm going to have to take this relationship one step at a time.

Dad moves to his spot in front of the television as soon as we're finished eating lunch. Sunday football begins in mere minutes, and Dad has his reading glasses on, his laptop in his lap, and papers spread across the coffee table. Dad has always been a huge sports fan, but his fanaticism has only increased with the invention of fantasy teams. He drives my mother crazy, but then Dad's put up with Mom's Elvis obsession for much longer. He's endured three trips to Graceland and who knows how many Elvis impersonators.

While Dad transitions into football land, Mom, Kennedy, and I get busy with cleaning up the kitchen. I wrote a blog last year about how a grilled meal can lead to an easy-to-clean kitchen. That isn't the case with this meal because Mom won't let her *good china* go in the dishwasher. It's fine, though. Better than fine, really. Kennedy seems nice and easy going. She doesn't have Hunter's intensity, which is a good thing.

We're still pretty quiet as we clear the table, Mom especially. She seems worn out. She's usually tired on Sunday; it's the only day that she and Dad both take off from the store. They close it on Sunday. Actually, the whole town is fairly buttoned up today. Mom seems exceptionally tired today. She wears a small smile on her face, but her tired eyes betray her.

"Mom, why don't you go lie down? Kennedy and I can take care of the dishes, and we'll be leaving soon anyway."

"You're leaving so soon?"

"Not leaving town, just going back to Hunter's place. There's some stuff that I need to do."

Mom reaches her hand out and squeezes mine. "If you want my opinion—which I'm sure you don't, but you know I'm going to give it to you anyway—I don't think you're in any kind of danger. I think that Hunter just wants you all to himself."

"Mom!" That just turns her tired smile into a real one.

"It's about time you two got together anyway."

My blush begins working its way up my neck.

"I haven't seen Hunter smile like that in ages." Now Kennedy's in on it, too.

"I have to ask." Mom's turn to embarrass me again. "That time that Hunter came to visit you, just before you went away to college." My eyebrow turns upward. Does Mom have to talk about this in front of Kennedy? Apparently, she does. "What was that about? Why wouldn't you talk to him?"

My cheeks flame with the heat of my blush. My face must be beet red at this point. Mom's expression makes it clear that I'm not getting out of this without a real answer. Where do I even begin?

I take a deep breath to buy some time. "Hunter and I had um...talked." *That didn't work. Way too obvious that it was more than talking.* Another deep breath. "At a party the night before." Mom tilts her head in a silent request to continue. "I knew I didn't hate Hunter at that point, but after talking to him that night, I wasn't sure how I felt. It was really confusing, and basically, I was too scared to talk to him then. I was leaving for college in a few days. The whole thing was just too much to handle."

Gosh. I sound like a selfish jerk. There's no telling

what Kennedy thinks of me right now. Her expression is thoughtful and doesn't give away any clue about what's going on in her head.

"I hated sending Hunter away that day. I felt certain that he wouldn't give up easily. He had quite a determined look in his eyes."

"There was a lot going on at our house around that time. Hunter took on a lot of responsibility."

Kennedy's words make me feel even worse. With all that Hunter had going on—working so much and watching many of us enjoy our summer and then excitedly leave for college—he didn't have time for me to be so selfish. He was better off without me, but he didn't deserve to have to worry about me along with all the other things he had to handle.

"I have been concerned about Thanksgiving. We've all grown very fond of you both." Mom gives Kennedy a heartfelt smile. She turns to me. "I didn't know if you and Hunter ever figured out your issues, but I never heard anything about the two of you talking after you went away to Texas. I figured that it might be a little awkward at first, but either you'd straighten things out, or at least you could agree that what happened between you was so long ago, that we could just move on." Her eyes study me. When I don't say anything, she continues. "So, which was it? Did you talk sometime after Hunter came to visit? Or, did you just decide enough was enough? Something had to happen for the two of you to be together now."

"Neither, really. Well, maybe it's that it's been a long time. Until the cabin Friday night, I hadn't seen or talked to Hunter since that time just before I left for college. But, even though my brain knew that I should be cautious, I just wasn't feeling it. Now, I don't know what I feel for him. I think I'm still coming to grips with the fact that Hunter isn't as bad as I thought he was. I figured that part out a long time ago, but I wouldn't let myself dwell on it." *That was an overshare.* The heat is back on my face. "Fate has brought us back together, though, and this time I'm not afraid of it. I'm excited to see what will happen."

"And so is Hunter," Kennedy says with a grin. "I haven't seen him like this...ever. It's about time, really."

"Okay. Enough of this conversation. Kennedy, you wash, and I'll dry?"

"You got it." Kennedy begins to fill the sink with water. She finds the dish soap too easily in Mom's Elvis soap dispenser, which means she's done dishes here enough times to know where to find it.

"I'm glad you're home, honey."

"Me, too. I've missed being here."

"Okay. I'm going to lie down. I will see you tomorrow."

"Goodnight, Mom. Thanks for a great lunch."

Mom gives us both one last smile before heading upstairs.

Chapter Twenty-Six

Hunter

It's surreal being here at the Franklin place two times in two days. I park my Jeep in the line of cars that's formed down the long dirt driveway. The ride here was silent. Brady is lost in his thoughts, and so am I. If I were a good friend, I'd spend more time worrying about Brady and what we might find here today. Instead, I can't stop thinking about Kate. I tried in vain to stay away from her, to protect myself from the devastation that she'll surely leave behind when she goes home to Texas. That didn't work out. Or, it did, depending how I look at it. Being with Kate is beyond anything I've even imagined over the years.

The other thing weighing on my mind is being back here at the Franklin place. I was too worried about Kate yesterday to let my feelings run amok. Now that Kate is safe and sound at her parent's house, I can't not think about the other times that I've been here.

When Dad would disappear, this is where I'd come to get him. Bobby Franklin was Dad's *connection*. Dad came here for weed at first, then weed wasn't enough. He was hurting, and I knew that, but drowning his sorrows in drugs was not the way to go. In the beginning, he would disappear for a few hours, and then it became longer. After a day or two, I'd come and get him. Usually Dad was all apologetic. He'd look at me with those sad eyes—the ones that look just like Kennedy's—and swear that he would never do this to us again. *But he did.* He somehow always found his way back to this house.

The ringing of my phone cuts through the silence.

"Hi, Granny. I only have a second to talk."

"I have a question." She pauses. This doesn't sound good. Granny doesn't hesitate about much of anything. "It's about Viagra." And there it is. My stomach turns as I do my best to block the mental images now threatening my subconscious.

"For the love of all that is sacred in the world, please do not ask me this question." Big sigh. "If Byron needs medical attention, please take him to the ER."

"It's more of a dosage question."

La la la la la la.

"Too much information, Granny. Please call a doctor or just...anyone else."

"Oh, be that way Mister High and Mighty." She disconnects.

I lean my head back against the seat and close my eyes.

"Your Granny and Viagra, huh?" Brady lifts his eyebrows as the corners of his mouth rise in a smirk.

"Don't remind me of that conversation. I'm trying to strike it from my memory." Deep breath. "So, are you quiet because you've got a lot on your mind, or are you pissed because I'm dating your sister?"

Brady scoffs. "Dating? Is that what you call it?"

"I don't know. I'd like to date her, and I did know Kate first. We have a demented history, but it's still a history." A long sigh escapes. "Besides, I care about Kate. I always have. You don't have to worry about me dumping her. She'll be the one to dump me when she goes back home."

"I guess." *Great. Did he have to agree so easily?* "Anyway, you can relax. I'm not thinking about you and Kate. I'm thinking about Jamie."

"I know."

"Was that whole *you could be in danger thing* an act to get my sister into your bed?"

"Of course not. I'm worried about both of you. We don't know who else is involved in this. There could still be other people who would like to make you and Kate forget everything you've seen."

"We haven't seen anything, and the people we have seen are either in jail or in the hospital."

"It's just an unknown."

Brady shrugs. "If you say so."

"You ready to go?"

Brady lets out a long sigh. "As ready as I'll ever be."

A group of men stand together near the house. Looks like just about everyone on our small force is here, as well as a few others from Charlottesville. Some of the locals who help out from time to time are here as well. Several in the crowd nod their hellos. A few speak. Chief Tisdale motions us over.

"Any word, Brady?"

"No, sir. I've looked all over for Jamie and called everywhere that I can think of. Where did you find her car exactly?"

"It's parked on a dirt road that can be accessed from Stagecoach Road. As the crow flies, it's only about a hundred yards that way." He points toward the back of the house. "Through those trees there. The FBI crime scene folks are going through her car now."

"Is there any sign of her at all? Have you been inside the house?"

"No sign of her, but if she's here, we'll find her."

The chief shifts his weight to his right foot. "We didn't go through the woods at all yesterday when we were here. We concentrated our search here at the house and outbuilding. We found no sign of Ms. Adams, but there wasn't much time to search before it got dark. There was an FBI team posted here last night. They didn't see anyone. A cursory search resumed this morning, and the car was found around noon. From the looks of things, the car wasn't parked there during the snowstorm on Friday night. It's a late-model Lexus SUV. There's plenty of road salt and dirt all over the red paint to indicate that the car had been out driving in the storm or shortly thereafter. There are a couple misshapen footprints near the car that are generally pointed in this direction. They fade into the muck of what was melting snow. It's a mud pit in places—so wet that any prints are long gone. We need to do a more thorough search of the woods."

Brady's skin takes on a green tinge. I give his shoulder a hearty pat.

"We'll find her." For Brady's sake and for all of us, please let us find her alive.

Brady nods his head. "Let's get started."

"Oh, no." Chief Tisdale uses his authoritative tone as he stares Brady down. It's hard to argue with him when he pulls that out. Brady opens his mouth to try, but the chief continues. "You will know when and if we find anything relevant to this case, but you are not participating in the search. If you take one step into those woods, I will arrest you. Have I made myself clear?"

"Yes, sir."

"Now, the rest of you, get moving."

The chief nods to Agent Cole, who begins giving orders. "Are you all familiar with this type of search?"

Everyone nods. We've all done this before, and recently even. There was a six-year-old girl lost in the woods near Wintergreen a few months ago. Fortunately, that search had a good outcome and she was found unharmed. Hopefully this one will, too.

Agent Cole continues. "We'll form our search line here at the start of the wooded area and move toward Stagecoach Road at the back of the property. Please call out if you see anything suspicious. We have the crime scene techs at the ready to check out anything and everything that you find. Focus on the big and small stuff. Nothing is too minuscule to check out."

The group begins walking toward the tree line. Brady stays put, as ordered. I give him a look that hopefully says *I've got your back*. There are enough of us that we can spread across the property line with about five feet of space between us. I'm in line between McMann and Parker. Parker just graduated from high school in May. He's wet behind the ears for sure, but he's a nice kid. He was on duty today, so he's wearing his uniform. He still looks a tad on the skinny side, but he's getting there. His olive skin and dark hair are a big contrast to McMann, the beach boy. No, McMann looks more like he's modeling for North Face today.

"I'm sorry about yesterday, man."

"What about?"

I think I know where he's going with this, but I'm not letting him get off easy. He knows it, too. His lips purse into a flat line.

"About Kate Richardson. I didn't know you were into her. I hear you two have a history. Didn't mean to step onto your turf."

Who says that? Still, I have to appreciate that McMann's backing off so easily. He's a good guy. He always has been. Well, always as in since I've known him. He moved here from New York three years ago. I just got a little carried away when I saw them together yesterday, probably because Kate was involved. Everything seems to be more intense when she's involved.

"Thanks."

"She's really something, isn't she?"

"Yeah." *That she is.*

Chapter Twenty-Seven

Kate

"Were you scared out of your mind?"

Kennedy and I are sitting on Hunter's couch, scarfing down pints of Ben and Jerry's. Kennedy's green eyes are wide with fright as I recount my story from yesterday.

"I was so scared. I didn't know what Brady had gotten himself involved in. It had to be serious for him to ask me to fly home to help him, but all I had was someone's make-up case. I didn't understand the enormity of the situation until I found diamonds. Then, I was practically hyperventilating, and, before I knew it, there was a gun in my face. I just kept thinking that I wished I'd told Hunter." I take a deep breath and let it out slowly so I don't hyperventilate now. Talking about what happened out loud is difficult.

"And Hunter rescued you?"

A small smile forms on my lips. "Yeah. I thought that I did a good job of hiding the bag and my reasons for being in town. Luckily, I'm a bad liar, or Hunter's really good at reading people. Whatever it was, Hunter knew that something was up, and he followed me. He saw me being taken by those men and rescued us."

The relief of that moment—the moment when Hunter's eyes met mine from across the room—washes over me. My eyes tear up as I remember the relief in Hunter's tight embrace.

"I'm sorry. I'm asking you all these questions about something that you don't want to talk about."

I wipe my eyes with the back of my hand. "It's okay. If Hunter hadn't been so *protective*, Brady and I might be dead right now." It's a chilling thought but true.

It's Kennedy's turn to sigh. "*Protective* is something that Hunter's very good at."

"Is that why you moved out of the house?"

She nods. "Yes. I couldn't take it anymore." She shoves another spoonful of New York Super Fudge Chunk into her mouth. Her eyes move to the fire for many seconds until she finally continues. "In most ways, Hunter couldn't be a better brother. He's taken care of me since Mom passed away. I was only seven.

Hunter was there for me then, and he's been there for me ever since. Brothers are territorial with their sisters, but Hunter's like a father, too. He's way too overprotective, and he's a policeman on top of that. When Johnny Haskins came to pick me up for the prom, Hunter actually showed Johnny his revolver and threatened him with it." My mouth opens in surprise. "I was so ticked." Kennedy smiles a huge smile, revealing her perfect teeth. "But, in that case, Hunter was right. Johnny tried to make it to second base before we even got to prom."

We both break out into giggles. "Brady's always been protective of me, too, but at least he's never threatened anyone with a weapon. Look how he was with Hunter today."

"It was a surprise to Brady that you and Hunter are together. Brady's a nice guy, but he seems kind of dense about those kinds of things. It was obvious to me that you two were hot for each other when I saw you last night at Minnie's." Now my eyes widen. Kennedy shrugs. "It was the way Hunter looked at you."

"We weren't even together yet."

"I could tell that, too. He looked at odds with himself, like he was fighting a losing battle. Then when you two walked into your parent's house today, I knew that he'd lost."

"*That he'd lost?* That doesn't sound good."

"Don't get me wrong. It's just that Hunter doesn't always see things as happily as other people might.

He had to deal with a lot of heavy stuff at a young age. I don't always understand him myself. It's obvious to me that he's totally in love with you. Maybe he just doesn't know how to deal with that."

"You think he's in love with me?"

"Oh yeah."

A knock at the door halts our conversation. Kennedy's smile falters. "Some bodyguard I am. I didn't hear anyone drive up." She moves quickly to a window and looks outside. "Great."

"Who is it?"

"You'll see."

She rolls her eyes in an exaggerated fashion and then opens the door to reveal a woman. She's about my age with short blond hair and light brown eyes. She's pretty, but has a weary, tired look about her. She holds a casserole dish out in front of her.

"Hi there, Kennedy. Is Hunter home?"

"Nope. He's not here."

"Do you know when he'll be back?"

"I don't. I'm keeping Kate company while we wait for him to get off work."

The woman peers inside. Her face tightens into a grimace when she sees me.

"Who are you?" she asks, her voice tight.

Kennedy answers for me. "Colleen Martin, this is Kate Richardson, Hunter's girlfriend."

Colleen's grimace turns into a full-on glare.

"Since when does Hunter have a girlfriend?"

"Since now."

Colleen speaks through gritted teeth. "Please tell Hunter that I came by." She exhales sharply, executes a neat military-type about face, and walks away from the door, casserole dish still in hand. Kennedy closes and locks the door.

"Who was that?"

"Someone who's been trying to get her claws into Hunter for way too long."

"Did she and Hunter ever go out?" The tightness in my gut takes me by surprise. I don't want to think about Hunter and Colleen together. I don't want to think about Hunter with anyone.

"Not that I know of. Hunter doesn't date a lot." She takes her seat next to me again. "Hunter never had much time for dating when he was younger. He certainly has the time now, but he doesn't go out at all. I've even wondered before if Hunter's gay."

Something like a chuckle or a gasp or maybe a combination of the two involuntarily leaves my throat. "Hunter's not gay."

Kennedy smiles a hugely wicked smile. "You would know."

"Why did you refer to yourself as a bodyguard earlier?"

"Hunter asked me to stay with you this afternoon."

"Oh." Just lovely. I thought we'd been having a great time together, and Kennedy's only here because Hunter asked her to be. "You don't have to stay with me. I don't need a babysitter."

"It's not like that. I promise." My forehead furrows. "Really. I'm having an awesome time. I don't get a lot of girl time. I'm too busy with school and work to hang with my girlfriends much, and I grew up with two brothers."

Kennedy does seem totally sincere. "But why would Hunter want you to stay with me? Just to keep me company?"

"I'm sure that's part of it, but part of his overprotective nature is that he's taught me to take good care of myself."

"What do you mean?"

"Like this." She leans over, picks up her purse, and takes out a small gun."

"You carry a gun?"

She shrugs and puts the gun back inside her bag. "Hunter started teaching me to shoot when I was twelve. He's made me practice several different safety exercises for different scenarios that could happen. He takes my safety very seriously."

"Have you ever had to use that?"

"Nope, and I really hope I never have to."

"You're amazing."

"Not really. Hunter's just made sure that I'm prepared for anything. In that way, he's a great brother."

I scrape my spoon around the bottom of my ice cream carton. How is this whole container gone? Did I really eat it all?

"Hunter usually means well, even when it doesn't

work out."

"What do you mean?"

"Like my bedroom. I'm sure you've noticed, especially being a designer and all, that this house is pretty plain. Hunter surprised me by painting my room pink. I came home from school on my eleventh birthday to find that Hunter and Justin had spent the afternoon painting my bedroom. They even used some stencil to paint the Eiffel Tower on one wall. It was so out of character for them and such a sweet gesture. They knew that pink was my favorite color and that I've always dreamed of going to Paris, but it's an awful shade of pink. It's the kind of thing that I would have loved when I was seven. I've had to pretend that I like it for years."

"Yeah. It's pretty bad." I can't help but let a little laugh escape.

"Please don't tell Hunter that I said that. It was so nice of him, and I was so touched by the gesture, but it's like living in a vat of cotton candy.

"Your secret's safe with me."

Chapter Twenty-Eight

Hunter

The woods on this property are way overgrown, making the search more tedious than I would have expected. Even during the winter when most of the brush is dormant, there are still enough briars and downed trees to make it slow going. We finish our search just before dusk. I heard a few of the searchers make calls during the day. We had nothing on our end of the property except for an old, empty plastic grocery bag that likely blew there from somewhere else.

I spy Brady as soon as I exit the tree line. He's standing next to an older gentleman near the porch steps. Thank you, God, for not letting us find Jamie in the woods. We'll be back tomorrow to search the surrounding area. I know that Brady needs some closure, but I didn't want to find her in these woods today.

"This is Hunter Simms," Brady says to the older guy. "Hunter, this is Tom Peterson, Jamie's Uncle."

We shake hands. "Nice to meet you, Mr. Peterson."

"Call me Tom, please. Thanks so much for your work out there today. I'm somewhat relieved that you didn't find her."

"Me, too, of course. Hopefully we'll hear from her soon."

He turns to greet McMann, which gives me time to study him further. He's around six feet tall with short, dark hair. He has a neatly trimmed mustache. It's not a full handlebar or anything, but it is still pretty substantial. His eyes are dark, but they're not black. There's some blue in there. Is it possible to have navy blue eyes? Whatever color they are, they are definitely full of worry.

"Do you live nearby?"

"I live in Richmond. The FBI found my phone number in Jamie's apartment and called me. It was such a horrible phone call to get, that Jamie's missing. It was the worst drive of my life, getting here."

Brady, as if reading my mind, says, "Tom last talked to Jamie about two weeks ago. He had dinner with her in Charlottesville in between her last two trips to Brazil."

"Yes. That Jamie. She spent a lot of time on the road lately, and the rest of her time with Brady here. It made it difficult to see her."

"How are you related to Jamie?" I can't resist asking, even if he has been questioned already.

"Technically, we aren't related. Jamie's family passed away in a car accident about five years ago. Jamie's father, Paul, and I grew up together. She's always been like a niece to me anyway and has always called me Uncle Tom. She's become family. I never married myself."

"What's going on over there?" McMann asks quietly. We all turn to see that many members of the search team have gathered near one of the FBI vans. "Let's go check it out."

I push my way into the small crowd clustered around the back of the crime scene van.

Bones. Lots of bones packaged in plastic evidence bags.

"We found a human skeleton earlier this afternoon. The body is fully decomposed—nothing to do with this case as far as we can tell—but we'll take it back to the lab to see what we can learn from it. All we can really tell so far is that it's from an adult male."

I study the bones laid out carefully in front of us. It's fascinating, really. Everyone else in the group thinks so, too. I've never seen a human skeleton outside of a museum. Something shiny catches my eye—a weathered metal chain and pendant in a clear plastic bag next to one of the larger bones.

"Fuck me."

"What the heck, Simms?"

"Was that found with the body?"

The crime tech looks slightly alarmed by my question. He nods slowly, never taking his eyes off me.

I take a deep breath and do my best to steady my wobbly legs. "How did he die?"

"We need to take him back to the lab to know for sure."

"You have a theory though. What is it?"

"There's some trauma on his skull. He could have been hit with something, or he could have just fallen and hit his head. There were a few fairly large rocks that were found near the body. It could have been a simple accident."

"He could have fallen in the woods and died out there? How long until you know?"

"It depends on the lab. There's no rush on this one. This skeleton is too old to be related to your case. It's been here for years."

"I know. Almost eleven years. This is my father."

Chapter Twenty-Nine

Kate

"Hunter!"

I jump off the couch and practically sprint to the front door. I stop short of hugging him. I want to, but something stops me. Whether it's the sadness in his eyes or the slump of his shoulders.

"Where's Kennedy? She was supposed to stay with you."

"I sent her home a couple hours ago. She left just before Brady called."

"She doesn't know?"

"No. I didn't think it was my place to tell her." *And I've been so worried about you.* Hunter gives me a nod of understanding and then just lets his head fall until his chin hits his chest. "Where have you been?" Please don't let me sound like a nag.

"I just drove around." Hunter raises his head. His eyes—light green now—meet mine. "I'm sorry if I worried you."

My heart melts. All that he's going through, and he's apologizing to me. My eyes moisten. Hunter's fingers move to my cheek as he gingerly wipes away a tear. He pulls me to him for a tight embrace. I hold onto him as tightly as I can. Thoughts fly through my head, so many of them, but I push them away. The only thing that matters now is Hunter and his pain.

Hunter pulls back enough for me to see his eyes, much darker now and full of emotion. His hand moves behind my neck. He holds it firmly and pulls me to him. His lips move hungrily over mine. His tongue demands entry to my mouth, and I open for him without hesitation. Hunter needs me right now, and I'm going to be here for him.

His hands move to my waist. He pulls me even closer until our bodies fit tightly together. There's no denying what he wants. I want it, too. His hands are now under my sweater, warm against my bare skin. He pauses there only briefly before pulling my sweater over my head. He deftly unclasps my bra and guides the straps down my arms. A growl escapes from deep in his throat before his mouth descends on my breast. My knees weaken. Hunter holds my waist again, this time for support to help keep me standing. He is not gentle with me, his touches and kisses hungry. He continues his onslaught of my breasts while he unbuttons my jeans and pushes them to the floor. My panties are next. I step out of them and stand totally naked before him.

His eyes, now dark and fiery with need, meet mine and hold. I take the hem of his sweater between my fingers and lift it over his head. His t-shirt is next. He kicks off his boots and removes his jeans and boxers. This is going fast, and I want it to be. I need him, and I need Hunter to know that I'm here for him. I kneel down on the floor in front of the fireplace. The warmth of the blaze washes over me and joins with the heat coming from Hunter. I lie back and open myself to him, giving him everything.

And that's just what he takes. His thrust is immediate, hard, and sure. *Incredible*. I angle myself upward slightly to catch all of him. Again and again he moves inside me in wonderful rhythm until I can't hang on any longer. He calls out my name as we climax together, and then he falls on top of me, breathless.

"Kate?"

"Yes?"

"I'm so sorry."

"For what?" It's not a good sign that he's apologized for something two out of the three times that we've made love.

Hunter sighs quietly and looks away from me. "For taking out my emotions on you."

"If that's what it feels like, you can take stuff out on me anytime. I'm glad that I'm here for you."

He leans toward me, and his lips brush mine.

"It's possible that my father didn't leave us."

"I know. Brady told me."

"I've hated him for so long, and I was wrong."

"No. You came to the only conclusion that you could have. How could you have guessed?"

"My last conversation with him was there. He and Bobby Franklin were sitting together on the front porch of the house. I don't know what Dad was on, but he was most definitely high on something. I could feel the anger in him as I moved up the walk. It was stabbing by the time I made it to the stairs. That should have been my sign to stay away, but I couldn't. I yelled at him. I told him what a horrible father he was to Kennedy and Justin. Sure, he was to me, too, but I was worried about them. They were younger. It was harder for them without a father and mother. The anger had been building up for a long time. Every time that Dad had gone away and come back. I resented the fact that I had to be the grown-up. All my friends were having the time of their lives, but I had to decline every invitation. All of my spare time was spent working to put food on the table for my family. I had to do that even when Dad wasn't out on some bender."

Hunter's eyes are full of tears. I don't know if they're tears of anger or tears of sadness or both, but they leak out of his eyes and fall down his cheeks. My fingers itch to wipe them away, but I don't dare move. Hunter has more to say. I can feel that he's working up to something bigger. So, I remain silent and let him talk.

"It was a warm fall day, you know, the kind of day where the sun shines strongly in the afternoon and then the temperature falls to chilly as soon as it sets. I didn't hold anything back. I told him what I thought of his parenting skills, and I told him how ashamed Mom must be up in Heaven. After Mom passed away, Dad started wearing her cross necklace. It was handmade by her Aunt Millie out of sterling silver and topaz. He usually wore the necklace under his clothes, but at that time, it was outside his t-shirt. When I spoke those words, the setting sun hit the cross just right to make it sparkle. It was like Mom gave me a sign that what I'd told him was true. Dad noticed that, too. He looked like I'd slapped him, but he didn't apologize. If anything, it was like the words made him stand firmer in his spot. Mr. Franklin cracked some joke, Dad laughed, and I left. I figured that he would come home whenever he came off his high. I even hoped that he wouldn't remember the awful things I'd said to him."

My hand intertwines with Hunter's. I can't not touch him. "He never came home. I've had to live the last ten years thinking, knowing, that I'm the reason

Dad didn't come home. I thought that my words had hit too close to home, and he was fed up. He didn't leave us."

I pull Hunter to me now and just let him cry. Shoot, I'm crying, too, crying my eyes out. I can't imagine the guilt that Hunter's been holding in all these years.

"Do they know how he died?"

"Not yet, but it could have been an accident. I knew it was him as soon as I saw that necklace. It has to be him."

I nod. Hunter would know. "I thought you said that your dad left just before graduation?"

Hunter sighs another hefty sigh. "That's what we told everyone. We had to. I wasn't eighteen yet, and I didn't want them to come and take Justin and Kennedy away. I'd been taking care of them by myself for more than a year at that point. I knew that it was up to me to take care of them with or without Dad."

"Oh, Hunter." I knew that he had a lot on his shoulders back then, but I never would have guessed that it was so much, too much for anyone to have to deal with, much less a teenager.

"Granny knew, of course, and she made sure that we were looked after, just like she always did. It wasn't hard to keep the secret. Dad didn't have a job, and he'd lost all his friends months before that. The only people who came looking for him were a couple of his druggy friends. You're the only person that

I've ever told this."

Tears spring to my eyes for another round of crying. He cares about me enough to tell me this. "I won't tell anyone."

"That's why I didn't try harder with you after that night in the closet. I got up the nerve to go to your house. I wanted to know if you felt the same way I did, but you wouldn't come to the door. I figured that told me enough. Even if you had come to the door, what did I have to offer you? Nothing. It was easy to convince myself to stay away from you after that."

"That's not true. I meant what I told you last night. That time with you in the closet terrified me. I was scared to death of how you made me feel and I wasn't willing to accept those feelings. I had already planned to go to Texas for school, but once I kissed you, I couldn't wait to leave. I practically ran away. You made me feel too unsettled. I just wanted safety and stability."

"Two things that I definitely couldn't give you at the time."

"True, but those things are overrated. Clint was safe, stable, and perfect for me on paper. I did love him, and we were talking marriage. Part of me thought he would be the perfect husband."

"This isn't helping."

"Let me finish. As I was saying, only part of me thought that Clint was perfect. There was another part of me—the part that got its way—that knew he wasn't right for me. I knew deep down that I didn't want safe and boring. Part of me remembered what it was like to kiss you. That spark was definitely something that I didn't have with Clint. I've only ever had that with you."

"I've never had that with anyone else. Of course, I haven't ever tried very hard to find it. I knew it was a lost cause."

"Yet you have women bringing you food. Colleen came by this afternoon."

"Colleen is just a friend. She lives down the road. We've never dated."

"Well she sure was unhappy to find me here. She didn't even leave whatever was in the dish she brought. She took it back home with her."

"Speaking of food, what is that amazing smell?"

"That would be the Frito Chili Pie that I made you."

"Where have you been all my life?"

Chapter Thirty

Hunter

"Is Brady pissed that I ditched him?" I wasn't thinking about the fact that I was his ride. Once I saw that cross pendant in the evidence bag, *I knew*. And I had to get out of there.

"No. Of course not. He understands. I sent him a text a little bit ago to let him know that you're back, and that you're okay."

"Is he coming back here tonight?"

"He's going to stay at his house. He thinks it's safe. Besides, he has Jamie's uncle with him. The two of them plan to team up to help find Jamie. What's the uncle like?"

"I don't know much about him. He's technically a

family friend. He lives in Richmond. He seems really worried about her, too."

We've finished eating. I had three servings of the most amazing Frito Chili Pie I've ever had. It's not like I'm a connoisseur or anything, but man, Kate's a good cook. Kennedy tried to cook for us, and while we appreciated her efforts, cooking is not her thing. At all.

"Thank you for cooking dinner. It was really great." But not as great as coming home to Kate. Her lavender scent, her warmth. I'm a goner for sure.

"Not too fancy for you."

"I'm such an ass. It's a miracle you're still here." I cover her hand with mine. "Thank you for staying."

"Chief Tisdale said that I have to stay, at least for now." A tinge of pink colors her cheeks. "Not that that's the only reason."

"I sure hope not."

"I'm not really in danger anymore, am I?"

"I don't know. Probably not, but as I'm sure Kennedy mentioned about a thousand times today, I'm overprotective of the people that I care about." *People I love is more like it.* It's too early for those words, but they aren't necessary to make Kate blush. Her face flushes right before my eyes.

A knock at the door causes Kate to jump. We both let out a laugh, but the moment is over. I pull back the curtain to see my neighbor, Sherri, of all people, standing at the door. *Crap.* She's seen me, so I have to open the door.

"Hi, Sherri."

She brushes past me into the living room. "I figure you've had dinner already, so I made you this apple..." her words fade when she sees Kate sitting at the table. "Who are you?"

Kate stands and walks toward us. "I'm Kate," she says politely, although her tone is tight. Kate doesn't take her eyes off Sherri.

"Kate, this is Sherri. She lives next door."

"I sure didn't mean to interrupt anything." Sherri begins backing toward the front door. "Y'all have a good night."

Sherri retreats completely and walks out the door. I give her a quick wave when she gets to her car. She does not wave back.

Kate folds her arms in front of her. "Your lady friends seem surprised to find me here." *Shit.* "Then, once they see me, they seem to take their food back home with them." A smile spreads across her face.

"She's not that great a cook anyway. Kennedy can't stand her."

"Kennedy and I had a really nice time today. We just hung out and talked, but she's really great. And, she thinks the world of you. You did a good job raising her."

My smile is cautious but involuntary. The words Kate's saying are exactly what I've always wanted to hear from her. Kate and Kennedy got along well, and of course, the big one—our first kiss rocked Kate's world as much as it rocked mine. Because now that

Kate is back in my life, I realize that I didn't keep my thoughts of her as suppressed as I had thought. There have been times when I thought about *what if?* Thoughts of that first kiss were on my mind a lot right after it happened. Once Brady and the Richardsons came into my life, it was torturous. The first time I had lunch at their house, Grace told me that Kate was practically engaged. It was all I could do not to drop my fork.

"What was it like the first time you had lunch with my parents?"

Can she read my mind? Nothing about Kate surprises me anymore.

"They're such nice people, and I was happy that they invited me, but it was so strange. The only time I'd been to their house was the time I came to see you." Driving over there was like reliving that day so long ago. It was awful. "Your mom remembered me. She mentioned to Brady that you and I went to school together. Brady already knew that, though. He is only a year older than we are. I wasn't sure if they remembered the sixth grade incident or not. I figured they had to, but they never made me feel uncomfortable about anything. It was so nice to be included in a family meal that I jumped at the chance to go back the next week. Justin was already in San Antonio, but once they found out about Kennedy, they insisted she come, too. They're such wonderful people."

"They're great. I miss them."

Then why don't you come back home? I can't say those words out loud, but the question is pretty obvious. She gets it, too. She blinks a couple times as the realization hits her, and then she averts her eyes.

"Has anyone learned anything from the men in custody? They're being questioned, right?"

"They are being questioned. The FBI might not necessarily share whatever they get from them, but I get the impression that they've gotten very little so far.

"Does the FBI know who they are or how they're involved in all of this?"

"The two men who were shot are brothers from near DC. They both made it through surgery but are still in the hospital in Charlottesville. They aren't talking, but we know who they are. They've both done time for theft, small stuff though. Nothing like diamonds. The other guy is David Justice. He's an environmental engineer and Jamie's boss. He doesn't have a criminal record. He's in FBI custody, and he's lawyered up, so I don't know how much information they're going to get out of him."

"Does the FBI think that Jamie was smuggling diamonds? That's why she was making all those trips to Brazil, right? The whole biofuel thing was just a cover?"

"Seems that way. Agent Cole was telling us today that there's a certification process that diamonds have to go through to be sold. There are a whole bunch of laws now that work to try to block the sale of conflict diamonds."

"Like blood diamonds? Do you think that's what these are?"

"Maybe. No one knows yet."

"Blood diamonds don't come from Brazil, though. They come from Africa."

"True, but maybe it's easier to get them to Brazil than to fly them directly to the US. The FBI still has a long way to go on this one, but they're working on it. They're trying hard now to find Jamie. She has the answers."

"Do you think she's alive?"

"I don't know, but it doesn't look good."

Chapter Thirty-One

Kate

Hunter's alarm blares at five-thirty. Normally, I wake up this early on my own, but Hunter kept me awake into the wee hours of the morning. Not that I'm complaining. *No way*. It was amazing—completely, totally, and utterly amazing. There were no more apologies from Hunter. There were only tender touches—okay, maybe not always so tender, but perfect nonetheless—and the fiery passion that I've been missing in my life.

"You're going to search for Jamie again?"

"Yeah. We didn't cover much ground yesterday afternoon, only the Franklin place. Today, we're planning to search the neighboring properties."

"Was there any evidence in her car that she was taken or that she was hurt?"

"I don't think so. I didn't hear of anything, but the FBI took her car back to the lab. Maybe I'll hear something new today."

"Can I go with you to help search? Are they asking for volunteers yet?"

"No, they aren't. I don't want to tell you what to do. I'm not that kind of guy. But, I am the kind of guy who worries about the people I care about. If I asked you to stay here with the door locked, would you do it?"

He cares about me. That's what my brain focuses on, not that he wants me to stay put. Hunter hasn't been so quick about getting my car back from the police station either. He might not have any control over that, or he might be trying to keep me safe. Who knows? Besides, other than one stop that I need to make, I don't mind staying here for the day. There's something I'd like to do.

"I can do that."

"Thank you," Hunter says with a grin. "Is it too much to ask for you to be waiting for me in this position when I get home?" The flush of my skin is hot and immediate. Hunter's grin grows. "I love it when you do that."

He kisses me lightly on my collar bone, and then I try my hardest to make him late for work.

❖ ❖ ❖

When I finally awaken for good, it's past eight, and the sun is shining brightly. I throw on my discarded pajamas and head for the kitchen. Coffee is the first thing on my agenda. I carry it with me to the couch and study the room around me. I'm painting Hunter's living room today. I want to do it for many reasons. First, it would really warm up the room if the walls were the right shade of gray. The gray would go well with the stones that surround the fireplace, the quilt that lies carefully folded on the couch where I placed it yesterday, and Hunter's eyes. My mouth forms a smile around my coffee mug. I don't usually match wall color to eyes, but hey, it works in this case. Is that why Hunter's mom chose those colors for his quilt?

I text Brady instead of calling him. I want to know how he's doing, but I don't want to interrupt him if he's at the search site, and he probably is.

How did things go with Jamie's uncle? I'm dying to know.

While I wait for his reply, I pour another cup of coffee and a bowl of Captain Crunch. I down that quickly and go for a bowl of Lucky Charms as well. I think I burned off enough calories for both boxes of cereal. A couple bowls won't hurt. I'm just finishing up when I finally get a reply from Brady.

Uncle is good. We're at the Franklin place again. Just waiting.

I text back a quick one.

Let me know if you need anything or hear anything. Love you.

Next on the agenda is a call to Mom. She usually takes Mondays off from the store, and Dad mans it by himself. They're slow days anyway, and Mom uses Mondays as her errand-running day. She answers on the first ring.

"Is everything okay?"

"Yes, I'm good." I can't imagine how Brady is right now with worrying about Jamie and what they might find, but I don't need to bring that up to Mom. "How are you feeling? Is your headache better?"

"Much better today. I think it was just from the stress of worrying about you two." That's probably true.

"Can you do me a favor today? My rental car is still at the police impound lot. Would you drive me to the station to get it? I'm stuck here at Hunter's house for the day, and I'm bored. I thought I might do some painting to give myself something to do."

"Sure, honey. I'll be by in an hour to pick you up."

"Perfect. Love you, Mom."

That's just enough time to shower and check my blog. I haven't posted anything since Friday morning, so I prepare a quick post about the Frito Chili Pie I made for dinner last night. Luckily, I thought to take a picture of it when it was just coming out of the oven. The last time I posted a southern recipe, Chicken and Dumplings, I had three comments from people in Europe telling me how much they enjoyed it. I'm always up for new things, and apparently many of my readers are as well.

The dark lines under Mom's eyes and the extra-cheery tone in her voice are dead giveaways that she isn't as good as she claims to be. But, I don't push her for details. She's worried about Brady and me. She worries about us on a normal day, but what's happened has thrown her into another orbit. Both her children were kidnapped and held at gunpoint. I can't even imagine what that would feel like.

"You look pretty happy, especially considering the events of this weekend. Things with Hunter must be going well."

I'm powerless to stop the smile that takes over my face. "Not *everything* that happened this weekend was bad. Hunter and I worked out some things."

"It's about time. He's grown into such a nice man."

Mom's talking about Hunter as a person, but my visions of *nice man* have more to do with his muscular chest and butt.

The receptionist, Dottie Matheson, is the only person that we see at the station. The place is practically deserted. Every available person is probably out searching for Jamie, and that's okay. Hunter's going to be mad enough when he finds out that I left his house, but I won't be out for long. Besides, this way he won't have to take me to get my car. We have *other things* to do anyway.

I've known Dottie practically my whole life. She and Mom went to school together. She asks questions about this and that as she's completing the paperwork to release my car. It feels like she's beating around the bush about something. Her fake surprised face gives her away. Here it comes.

"I hear that you and Hunter Simms are an item now." She just makes the statement and lets it hang there as she studies my response. Keep breathing steadily. Are my pupils dilating?

"Where did you hear that?"

"I ran into Sherri Thompson this morning at the Kroger. Sherri told me that you and Hunter were having dinner together last night at his house." Dottie's tone isn't negative, just matter of fact, like she's testing out the rumor she heard to see if there's any truth to it. Still, I don't want to give her any more information.

"We did have dinner together last night." And I'm staying at his place. That part I can keep to myself for now even if the word will get out eventually. This is a small town. It's hard to keep anything a secret.

"I think that's lovely. Hunter is a good catch. He's had a hard life and deserves some happiness. Don't you think so, Grace?"

"Definitely." Mom jumps right into the conversation like she couldn't wait to give her opinion on the matter.

Dottie gives me the keys to my rental car before hugging us goodbye. Before I walk to it, however, Mom and I head down to the store to see Dad. I was so nervous when Hunter and I made this walk on Saturday afternoon. This time I'm filled with the excitement that a trip to Richardson's General Store has always given me.

Dad shouts a greeting to us as soon as we enter. The sweet cinnamon scent hits me hard. How could I have stayed away from here for so long? It isn't just the store, it's all of it. Mom, Dad, Brady...Hunter. It's time for me to come back home. Hunter's right. I can do my job from anywhere. Sure, I've made a life for myself in Austin, but Hunter isn't there. He's here. My family's here.

Ironically, I think Hunter is the reason that I stayed away from Davidson for so long in the first place. Well, sort of. In my defense, I didn't know that's what I was doing. I planned to go to the University of Texas because it was a good school, it was far from home, and they accepted me. I had this big urge at the time to go away to school. I didn't hate life in Davidson, but I wanted to spread my wings. Mom and Dad finally agreed and paid the tuition, but as the time to leave got closer, I became more frightened. Major doubts were plaguing me about going so far away from home for college. I hoped it was just cold feet, but then again maybe a school a couple hours away from home would have been far enough.

Then there was that kiss. Hunter's kiss turned my world upside down, but it was more than that. What it did was, well, it scared the crap out of me. So much that I couldn't wait to get away from this place and away from Hunter. Now, he's one of the biggest reasons that I want to be back home.

I know exactly what I'm going to do.

The giddiness marches down my spine like an ice cream freeze. *I'm moving back to Davidson.*

Sure, I will miss the friends I've made in Austin, but Davidson is where I need to be. My family is here. The store. The man I love.

Hunter doesn't need to know about this decision right this second—talk about running for the hills to escape the clingy female. We've already covered a ton of ground in a couple days. I don't need to push my luck. He wants me to stay until Thanksgiving. We can see how he feels about me then. Baby steps. Just because I've realized how much I love him doesn't mean that Hunter's realized he feels the same way about me. *I love him.* The realization fills me, making me whole for the first time in my life. This is what I've been missing. I've been too stupid to realize it. Hunter can have all the time that he needs to hopefully come to the same conclusion.

"Mom, Dad? I've got to run." I give them both quick hugs.

"What's the big hurry? You just got here."

What is the big hurry? I don't know. It's as if now that I know what I'm going to do, I'm itching to get it done.

"I just have a lot to do today. I'll call you later."

My bouncing stride back to my car leaves me almost dizzy. I can't wipe the smile off my face. *I'm moving back home.* It's all I can do not to shout the words down Main Street.

Chapter Thirty-Two

Hunter

I don't want to be here.

That plays a lot whinier when my mind speaks the words over and over. I'm not usually one to get out of work or complain. Today is different. Kate is home—possibly, although not likely—lying in my bed waiting for me. She isn't the kind of woman to lie around in bed all day, but this is my fantasy. Maybe I wore her out with our lovemaking last night, and she's been home resting up for tonight. The exhaustion has me repeating my whiney phrase over and over. *I don't want to be here.* I'm exhausted for sure, and walking around the woods all day isn't helping.

Fantasy over.

Kate lives halfway across the country. My daydreaming about her at *home* isn't a reality. My home isn't hers. The remaining happy feelings crash and burn. Shoot, she's not here for much longer, and at some point, she'll go stay with her parents. She's only with me because she could be in danger. But, even I have to admit that the longer this goes on, the more likely it is that she's not in any danger at all.

Jamie, however, is in a whole lotta trouble whether we find her alive or dead. I pray we find her alive for lots of reasons, most of which have to do with her explaining herself to Brady. We've walked through forest and field in the freezing cold and haven't found a clue to her whereabouts. The search is taking its toll on all of us. We slowly walk our line as we scour the ground for anything that might be out of place.

Man, I thought I was tired. Brady sits on the tailgate of a pickup with Jamie's uncle. Chief Tisdale stands next to them. The bags under Brady's eyes are darker and even more pronounced. What would it be like if I were in his shoes right now—to find out that the woman you've been dating used you? Did Jamie ever like Brady at all? He's a good guy, the best friend in the world, and the kind of guy that would do anything for you. Did Jamie search him out from the beginning just for that reason?

Brady stands and walks to meet me as we approach. "Jamie's Uncle Tom bought lunch for everyone. There are sandwiches and drinks over there." He points to boxes that sit in the tailgate of a nearby truck.

Tom shrugs his shoulders. "It's the least I could do to thank you."

I grab a sandwich and sit with Brady and Tom. There's nothing on my phone from Kate—not a text or a voicemail. *Nothing.* She probably figures that I can't use my phone while searching, but that doesn't help the disappointment. Maybe I really have been living in a fantasy world the last couple days.

"Have you heard anything from Kate?" Probably not good to bring up our relationship—if it could even be called that—to Brady, but I need to know.

"She texted me earlier to see how I was. That's it."

"Did she say what she's doing today?"

"Don't you know? She's at your house. Text her yourself and leave me out of it."

"Kate is your sister, Brady?" Brady nods his answer to Tom's question, his annoyance clear. "Why is she staying with Hunter?" As soon as the words are out of Tom's mouth, his expression turns sheepish. "Oh. So sorry. That's none of my business. Just trying to get a handle on who everyone is—how they're involved with Jamie's disappearance."

"Kate's the one I called to retrieve Jamie's make-up bag, the one with the diamonds."

Tom's expression turns thoughtful. "Kate found the diamonds before she met with the kidnappers, didn't she?"

"Yes."

"I'm not trying to speak badly of your sister, but is it possible that Kate was the one who skimmed off some of the diamonds? Maybe she took a few for some reason—whether for herself or to give to the police as evidence—and that's where the missing diamonds are."

"Kate would never do that, and besides we're not even sure that there are missing diamonds."

I'm done with this conversation. The mere suggestion that Kate would keep the diamonds for herself is pissing me off.

My opinion must be evident because Tom's eyes widen. He back pedals immediately. "It was just a thought. I didn't know if anyone had addressed that possibility."

It's true that I hadn't thought of it, but there's no way in hell that it could ever be true. Enough of this conversation. Without another word, I take my sandwich to an isolated spot and stand alone. The ground is too wet to sit. Big sigh. *Screw it.* I don't want another bite. The sandwich is cold just like the asshole who bought it.

Geez, I'm really in a mood here. I would likely feel better if I could talk to Kate.

Do not call her.

The last thing I want to do is pressure her. Kate should set the tone. It has to be enough that she's staying with me while she's here. It has to be enough that I will have the memories of us together when she goes back home. There will be no reminders of her around my house. There will be many memories, but after a while, those will dull and so will the scent of lavender that seems to have permeated my home.

Maybe Kate's written something on her blog. *Geez, I'm like a stalker.* I bring it up on my phone anyway. It isn't something that I check daily, but I do look at it from time to time. A photo of last night's dinner is the first thing to come up. She has posted today. It's weird to see something she made just for me out there for the world to see.

Maybe Kate didn't make it just for me.

The thought is like a stab in the gut. *She did.* I know she did. Didn't she?

Shit, this sucks.

The buzz of my phone brings me out of my thoughts.

Thank you, God. Kate's finally calling me.

It isn't Kate. The station's main number is displayed on the screen.

"Hi, Dottie. What's up?"

"Just wanted to see how things are going there."

"Nothing to report so far."

"The chief just told me that you were breaking for lunch, so I thought it would be okay to call." So you should have known that there is nothing to report here. What's this call really about?

"Okay."

"Now, I don't mean to be nosy and in your

business." Yes, you do. You are constantly in my business and everyone else's, no matter how well-meaning your intrusions. "But, I saw Grace and Kate Richardson this morning. That Kate is such a lovely young woman, and I'm so happy for you. I couldn't wait to tell you."

Wait. What? "You saw Kate? At the station?"

"Yes. She came by this morning to pick up her car from the impound lot."

Shit.

"What exactly did Kate tell you about us?"

"She only confirmed that you two had dinner together last night. I can tell, however, that there's more to the story. I wasn't born yesterday, you know. You two are good together."

Now if only Kate would figure that out.

"Thank you, Dottie." What else do I say in response to that? "Anything else?"

"Watch it smart ass and learn how to take a compliment."

"Can we talk about this later?"

"Oh, we will. You can count on that."

"Thank you, Dottie. You know I love you."

"Love you, too, sweetie, which is why I'm going to give you some advice. Take her out somewhere nice tonight and buy her flowers."

"Yes, ma'am."

I disconnect with Dottie and let her words wash over me again. Kate left the house. She agreed that she wouldn't, but she did, and she now has her car. It was childish of me to keep her car locked up longer than necessary, but she didn't have to run out and get it at her first opportunity. *Sonofabitch*.

I dial Kate's number anyway, even though I said I wouldn't and even though my brain is telling me that this is a huge mistake. I can't stop myself. She makes me crazy.

Chapter Thirty-Three

Kate

A smile breaks out spontaneously at the sight of Hunter's name on my call screen.

"Hi." Hunter speaks only one word but the emotion behind it is intense. *Smile gone.*

"Did you find her?" The words come out as a squeak. Poor Brady.

"No. We haven't found anything."

Relief.

"What has you so upset?"

"Why did you go get your car? You said that you would stay at the house? Where are you now?"

Too many questions.

"I'm at your house. I only went out to get my car."

And one other tiny stop. "Mom took me. I know you're really busy working on this case, so I didn't want to put you out. I don't want to pay for a rental car to have it just sit in some police lot." It's silly, but even if it's just sitting in front of Hunter's house, at least I can see it there. "I did tell you that I would stay here, and I mostly have. I'm not a prisoner, you know. I can come and go as I please."

Even knowing that I shouldn't let Hunter's overprotective tone tick me off, it still rubs me the wrong way.

"And what about your blog post this morning?"

"What about it?"

"You acted like you made that dinner for me, but that wasn't what it was about, was it? You made dinner for you so that you would have something for your stupid blog."

Shut up.

He did not just say that.

My eyes take in the current condition of Hunter's living room. The furniture is moved away from the walls. The room is taped, and half of the long wall is the perfect shade of gray. The rocks I gathered from the stream outside are in the dish on the coffee table. I was planning to post the before and after shots of this paint job, just to show how much a coat of paint can change a room, but I'll be damned if I'm doing this project for my blog. I'm doing this for Hunter, the idiot. He's the one who told me to find projects in Davidson so that I could stay here until

Thanksgiving.

A couple deep breaths settle some of my nerves. The time does nothing for Hunter though. I can feel his anger coming at me through the phone.

"We should finish this conversation in person. I don't appreciate you calling just to yell at me."

"Fine." Really? That's what he's going with? Two can play at that game.

"Fine."

Hunter disconnects, leaving me to stare blankly at my phone. Is this our first fight as a couple? I'm not sure what's behind it, but I'm okay with it if we get to have angry make-up sex.

I've just wrapped up the painting when Kennedy knocks on the door. She wears her Minnie's uniform and carries a takeout bag.

"You're an angel with perfect timing. Besides the fact that I'm starving, you can help me move the furniture back."

Her gaze takes in my work, and she laughs out loud.

"What's so funny?"

"Does Hunter know that you did this?"

"No."

"Good luck with that."

"You don't like it?"

"I love it. Hunter's just not so big on change."

Just what I need, another thing for Hunter to be mad about. I'm already bothered by my conversation with Hunter and now there's the fact that I know that Kennedy's father didn't leave them, and I can't tell her. Now, I get to worry that Hunter will be upset about my painting, too. Let him be ticked. I'm in his life now, and there are going to be changes. He's going to have to learn to deal with them.

Lunch with Kennedy is great. She brought us both meatloaf, mashed potatoes, and corn. *So good*. Kennedy's so easy to talk to. It's like having a sister, but we're old enough that we get to bypass the years of fighting that would have happened if we had grown up together.

"This is really fun, but I have to go soon."

"What are you doing today?"

"On Mondays, I work at Millie's for breakfast and lunch. Then I try to get some homework in before my classes. I have two classes on Monday nights."

"College was hard enough for me without working a part-time job. Hunter must be so proud of you."

Kennedy blushes slightly. She might be blushing a lot, but it's not so obvious with her olive skin. My blushes are like a flashing light. Kennedy has a rosy tint to her cheeks.

I push back from the table and hug my stomach. "Lunch was so good. I don't know the last time that I had meatloaf."

"For me it was last Monday. I eat most of my

meals at Millie's, which is good because I can't cook to save my life, and Granny isn't so great at it either."

"A grandma that can't cook. That's a strange concept."

"You have no idea."

"I kind of do, actually. I was with them Saturday night, remember? Your granny and Byron couldn't keep their hands off each other."

"Don't I know it? Byron stayed over last night. I found his teeth in a cup next to the kitchen sink this morning. Not what I needed to run into at five-thirty in the morning."

Maybe not, but we bust out with laughter anyway. A knock at the door doesn't stop the giggles. They don't stop until I pull back the curtain and see a woman looking back at me through the window.

Really! Another one?

This has got to stop.

I wrench the door open and stare her down. She's close to my age—thirty tops. She has long brown, almost black hair and deep brown eyes. The most striking feature is her skin, which is completely flawless as far as I can tell. Not a freckle or mole to be seen. *Bitch*.

"Can I help you?" She does not carry a dish or anything else in her hands. "Let me guess, you have a whole meal in your car, and you need Hunter's big strong muscles to help you carry it inside."

"Excuse me?"

Kennedy's with me now. "You're new. What do

you want with my brother?"

"Look, I have no idea what you're talking about. My car broke down near the end of your driveway. I was just wondering if I could borrow a couple tools and maybe a flashlight."

"Do you know how to fix it? My brother has made sure that I know a lot about cars. I'd be happy to take a look."

"No." Her face reddens in response to her outburst. Her hands come together, her fingers fidget as she backpedals. "That's very kind of you, but I can manage."

"We can see what's in here." I point to Hunter's toolbox resting on the floor near the door. Now that I've called this poor woman names—sure, they were in my head, but I still wasn't very nice to her—I need to make up for it. I don't need that kind of bad karma out there in the universe trying to get back at me.

The woman steps across the threshold into the house. I get a closer look. Her hands are trembling. She's flustered, and it's no wonder. Her car broke down, and on top of that, I was terrible to her, thinking that she was one of Hunter's admirers.

The woman stands as if she's expecting me to hand her the toolbox, but I can't do that. I need to go above and beyond now after the way I treated her. I kneel next to it and open it up. It's a large case with most of the tools held in their own foam cut-out.

"Here's a flashlight." I move to take it out of its slot.

"Wait!" The woman's voice is so loud that I jump. Kennedy does, too. "Can I just borrow the whole box? I'll bring it right back. I promise."

"Sure."

I don't know why I feel compelled to remove the light, but I do. I power it on to verify that it works. The light shines from the end of the metal rod and reflects off of something inside the case.

Diamonds.

My stomach squeezes. There are diamonds resting in the cutout where the flashlight was being held. There aren't many, maybe seven or ten. Enough to know that these are the missing stones. My stomach tightens, the meatloaf threatening to revolt.

"You're Jamie, aren't you?"

Jamie's supposed to be blond, but that's easy enough to change. I look up at her, and—no surprise here—she now holds a gun out in front of her, her hand shaky. She steps backward so that she can train the gun on Kennedy as well. Jamie's face is no longer smiling and apologetic. Her mouth takes a firm line. Her eyes narrow.

"You couldn't just give me the case, could you? You and your brother are just too fucking helpful."

"Don't you talk about Brady like that, you bitch." *Probably not a good idea to call someone a name if they have a gun pointed at your face.* Jamie rolls her eyes, so I continue. "He's one of the few nice guys left, and you just used him."

"I won't deny it. I chose Brady for that very

quality. I had to do something. I was desperate, and he did his job nicely. It would have worked out very well if they hadn't already been onto me. I was worried about the cop that moved into the apartment next door to mine. I thought he was there to watch me, and I needed a safe place to keep the diamonds. That's where Brady worked perfectly. He had no idea that he stored the diamonds for me at his house from time to time. The run last week was supposed to be my last. I was going to hand the majority of the diamonds over on Friday at my usual drop and then leave town. They never counted them in front of me. I'd never been caught when I took one or two of the diamonds, so I thought I could get away with taking ten. Of course they'd count them at some point, but I'd be in St. Maarten before they figured out what I'd done."

"How did you know on Thursday that there was a problem?"

Jamie stands a little straighter and looks down her nose. I don't expect her to answer my question, but she does.

"There was a car following me. The driver kept a couple cars in between us, but he followed me from my apartment to my office. That was too much of a coincidence. So, I called Brady and asked him to hide the diamonds. I didn't tell him about the overflow that I'd put in his toolbox. There was no need. I had a key to his house and could come back to get those later."

Geez Brady. You gave her a key to your house already.

Keep her talking.

"But they knew about Brady, didn't they?"

"Yes. I thought I'd covered my tracks there. They were never supposed to know about him, but they did. I left at lunch on Thursday, and although it took a little maneuvering, I lost my tail. That's when they knew something was up, and they started following Brady."

"And you left him high and dry"

"Not exactly. I knew that they were using that old farmhouse. I hiked in from the back and saw that they had Brady tied up in the house. From what little I overheard, they didn't have the diamonds. I assumed they were looking for me at that point. I parked my Lexus near the house in the hopes that the police would find the car and start looking for me nearby. Then they would find Brady and rescue him. I walked four miles back to town Saturday morning to buy a new car."

"That sort of sounds like you were trying to help Brady."

"I wanted to do something for him. I did feel badly about getting him wrapped up in this mess. He's a nice guy, but he's also the moron who got my diamonds stolen."

Anger burns in my gut. I should be scared that there's a gun pointed at me. Instead, I'm fired up. What can I do about it? I can't fight her. I'm not armed.

But Kennedy is.

Kennedy's purse is hanging on the arm of the chair. Kennedy's eyes are clear, her face set in concentration. She's already on it. She's even inched a little closer to her purse. It won't be easy to get that far though. Jamie will notice that something is off.

I take a step in the opposite direction, toward the couch.

Too obvious. Jamie raises her gun a little higher.

"Don't move."

I steady my hands in an effort to make her see that I'm not going to move, but I don't move back to my original spot. I can keep Jamie talking. Maybe if her attention is on me, then it won't be on Kennedy. Kennedy is young and gorgeous. She doesn't look like she'd be any kind of threat to anyone. She especially doesn't look like someone who would carry a pistol in her purse.

"Why didn't you go back for the diamonds in the toolbox?"

"I did." Her eyes flash with annoyance. "I couldn't risk going to Brady's on Thursday night. I was a nervous wreck and spent the night in a motel in Lynchburg. I bought new clothes and hair color and changed my appearance and went to Brady's place on Friday night during the ice storm. I walked there from a few streets over, carefully watching my back the entire time. There was nothing. No tool box.

Thursday morning it was there on the living room floor. By Friday night, it was gone. It took me a while to figure out what might have happened to it."

Thank goodness Jamie's a talker. Maybe it's because she's been alone for a couple days, or maybe she just feels like she has to get all this off her chest. Whatever the reason, she's spilling her guts and focused on me, and Kennedy is inching closer to her gun. She's covered about half of the eight or so feet she has to travel, but the farther she gets from us, the more obvious it's going to be that she's up to something. Plus, I know deep down that it's a bad thing for Jamie to tell us everything. Does that mean she's going to kill us after she confesses?

"Then it finally hit me. Brady told me once that he wasn't very handy. He said that he didn't even own a wrench. So, it made sense that he had to have borrowed that toolbox from someone, and his best buddy, Hunter, seemed like the best place to start."

"Quite a mess you've gotten yourself into, Jamie."

We all look at the door to see another gun pointed at us. It's a much bigger gun and held by a man who looks like he means business. A wave of nausea crashes over me. There's no way I'm back-talking this guy. I want to make eye contact with Kennedy, but I don't dare. Based on the fear now clearly emanating from Jamie, we're in deep trouble.

"Put your gun down, Jamie. Now."

She slowly lowers her gun to the ground and backs away from it to stand next to me. *This is so bad.* The mystery man is focused on the two of us. I don't dare look in the direction of Kennedy. Why hasn't he looked at Kennedy?

It's the front door. It's blocking his view of Kennedy.

He can't see her!

"Tom, let me explain."

"Tom? Are you her uncle, or family friend, or whatever? The one that's been staying with Brady?"

The man smiles a sinister smile that even shows in his eyes *Creepy.*

"I am a *friend* of Jamie's. I've been very concerned with her well-being and the well-being of my diamonds. Now, where are they?"

I have to buy more time for Kennedy. She's our only hope. Keep him talking.

"That was awfully brave of you to go to the police. Weren't you concerned that they might catch onto you?"

He sighs heavily. "I don't have time for your amateur hour. Give me the diamonds now."

The sound of the shot is deafening. Tom's eyes freeze in place. His entire body stiffens. He drops the gun as his body falls to the ground as if in slow motion. Blood runs onto Hunter's beautiful wood floor in a line and then forms a pool about six inches from his chest. It's mesmerizing.

"Don't even think about it."

Kennedy is next to me now. The gun is still in her hand and now pointed at Jamie. Jamie's gun lies on the floor not far from her reach. She looks back at us with sad eyes.

Chapter Thirty-Four

Hunter

Brady holds on to the door handle as I round the turn into my driveway. I don't think I've ever driven this fast. My gut clenches at the sight of the ambulance, lights flashing. Kate and Kennedy are okay—I know that—but it doesn't change the fact that they could have been killed. The two people I love the most killed in my own home. My forehead instantly dampens. I shove the gearshift into park and all but leap from my Jeep.

Kate sits on the bottom porch steps.

She really is okay.

She hops down the steps and into my arms. I pull her to me. Hard. My nostrils fill with her lavender scent. My eyes moisten and before I know it, I'm full-on crying. I don't care. I love this woman, and I don't care who knows it. My life would have been decidedly different if I'd had this attitude back in the sixth grade, but fate made sure that I got the girl anyway, even if it took its own sweet time to make it happen.

I pull back enough to look at Kate. She's crying, too, her cheeks pink from the effort.

This is the moment, the one where I should tell Kate that I love her. *I do love her.* I always have, and this would be the perfect time to tell her. But, the words are stuck in an emotional knot in my throat. I swallow hard and almost choke on the reality that the words won't come.

The people I love leave me.

The words will have to wait because they are clearly not coming right now. The moment is gone. I will tell her later when we're alone. I have to come clean about how I feel about her.

Kate's lips graze mine lightly. "Let's go inside so you can see Kennedy. She's okay."

She takes my hand and pulls me around the side of the house and through the kitchen door. A woman who must be Jamie is handcuffed and sits at my kitchen table with Matt Parker. Most of our department was out looking for Jamie's body. If Kennedy hadn't taken care of this Tom Peterson guy, then it might have been in the hands of our youngest patrolman. Something to think about in the future.

I see now why we didn't come through the front door. Uncle Tom lies dead in the doorway.

Kate pulls me into my living room—at least I think it's my living room. It looks a lot grayer than it did when I left for work this morning. Kennedy sits on the couch in front of the newly painted wall talking with Bryce Chambers, one of our younger recruits. She's pale, but she seems okay otherwise.

I exhale a huge breath that I didn't even realize I was holding.

Relief.

Kennedy stands and hugs me warmly. Chambers smiles from ear to ear as he looks at Kennedy.

"Your sister is amazing, Hunter. She took the guy down in one shot."

Kennedy smiles shyly, as if she's unsure how to take Chambers's praise. Deep breath. Kennedy is amazing, but that doesn't mean I want her socializing with the likes of Chambers. She's going to college. There's no time for her to fall in love and mess up her plans. I open my mouth to tell her so, but the words don't form before Kate turns me toward her. The look in her eyes clearly commands me to shut my mouth, so for now, I do.

Brady joins us and pulls Kate into an embrace.

"I'm so sorry, Kate. You, too, Kennedy. If it hadn't been for my stupidity, none of this would have happened."

Kennedy touches Brady's arm and gives him a smile. "We're fine, Brady. None of this was your fault."

Brady's gaze finds Jamie. He walks over to her, and I follow. Brady isn't irrational or aggressive, but I want to be his wingman here, just in case. I can't let this situation get any worse for him than it already is.

Jamie looks a lot different than her photo. The change to her hair color is striking. What used to be blond is now a dark brown. She also looks beaten down and exhausted. Maybe the days of running have taken their toll. That's fine with me. She deserves that and whatever punishment she's going to get at the hands of the legal system.

Brady's hands move to his hips as he stands near her. His gaze is thoughtful. The room is silent as we wait for Brady to start his tirade. He doesn't. When he does finally speak, his voice is calm.

"Was I just part of your plan all along?"

Jamie doesn't look away, I'll give her that. "I did target you in the beginning as someone who could help me. You are so kind." She keeps eye contact, her eyes clearly sorrowful. How much of this is an act, we'll never know. She's already proven herself to be quite the little actress. "I did grow to really like you, though. If this had gone on longer, then I could have grown to like you a whole lot. I'm sorry for what I did to you. I never meant to hurt you. If Tom hadn't been on to me, this could have ended differently."

Brady shakes his head. "No, I'd say this ended the right way. I do wish that I would have caught onto you and your not-uncle Tom. You hurt my family."

Brady sighs and heads down the hallway toward the back of the house.

"Where do the diamonds come from?" She'll be asked this question by others, but I want to know.

"Africa." The *duh* is very evident in her tone, even if she doesn't actually say it. I'm sure she didn't act like this around Brady, but what a bitch.

"Isn't there paperwork and certifications involved with selling diamonds?"

She shrugs. "They're paired back together at some point down the line and sold as legitimate. I did my part—getting the diamonds from Brazil to the U.S."

My questioning is over. The room now fills with more law enforcement people than I would think could fit in my house. The cavalry has arrived.

Chapter Thirty-Five

Kate

There are entirely too many people in Hunter's home, and I think I've been questioned by every one of them. It sure feels that way. The adrenaline of those moments has long since gone, and I've had plenty of downtime in between interviews to realize that I could have been killed today...again. Kennedy, too. Kennedy's quick thinking saved us, but the cost is likely to be very high, for her especially. She killed a man. Even in self-defense, that has to take an enormous toll on a person.

I've asked about Kennedy throughout the afternoon, but I haven't seen her in hours because the FBI agents separated us right away. They put me in her bedroom. I'm not sure where Kennedy is. We need to make sure that we're here for her, and we will be.

We.

Me and Hunter.

Does Hunter think of us as a *we?*

The rap on the door doesn't surprise me, but what does is that it's Granny who walks inside. She immediately hugs me.

"Look at you." She squeezes a little tighter, her scent of peppermint candy filling my senses. "Thank the Lord that you two are safe. Hunter's finally in love. Or, maybe I should say in love again. Don't go and get yourself killed now." A mangled giggle makes its way from my throat. Even now, Hunter's Granny can make me laugh. She untangles me from her grasp and pulls me down onto the bed to sit beside her. My hand remains between both of hers. "You laugh, but it's true."

"I love Hunter. I want to believe that he loves me, too." Granny squeezes my hand. "Sometimes I'm sure that he does, but other times...not so much." Like when he has the perfect opportunity to tell me, and he just doesn't. Hunter's embrace outside today told me that he loves me, but he didn't say the words. Am I silly for wanting the words?

"Here's the thing about Hunter. He's had a rough time, and he's had to do a lot of things on his own. I've watched him handle his mother's passing, and then his father's leaving." I start at her words. Does she know that her son didn't leave his children? "Hunter told me about finding the bones out in the woods and that it was likely an accident. It will be good for Hunter, Justin, and Kennedy, to have some closure about their father, but the truth is that whether he actually ran off or not, their father still left them. He picked the numbness of the heroin and whatever else he was using over the responsibility of raising his children. That's too much for a young man to have to deal with. He does love you though. I know that for certain, and you know it in your heart."

Granny's right. I do know it. We are a *we*.

I stand and stretch. "I need to get out of here for a while. Thank you for this."

She stands and brings me to her again for a quick hug. We walk out into the living room together. The law enforcement personnel have thinned out. Chief Tisdale stands in the kitchen talking on his cell phone. He nods and disconnects when he sees me.

"Would it be okay if I go for a drive? I just need to get some fresh air."

"That would be fine, Kate. You've been through enough today."

"Want me to come with you?" Kennedy looks at me with expectant but exhausted eyes.

"No, thanks. Not this time. I just want to be alone for a little while." I grab my purse off the coffee table and head for the door. "Be back soon."

Hunter stands outside talking to Officer McMann.

They both look at me.

Officer McMann smiles. "Alright, Hunter. I'm out of here. See you soon Ms. Richardson."

I nod in his direction without taking my eyes off of Hunter.

"Are you leaving?" His expression is unreadable, but his tone is not a happy one.

"I'm just going for a drive to clear my head." He sighs as he folds his arms across his chest. "You do the same thing. I have a lot on my mind right now. I'm thinking of moving home to Davidson. What would you think of that?"

I had planned to think about this some more before springing it on him, but this is as good a time as any to talk about it.

Hunter stands a little straighter. "I don't believe that you could give up your fancy life in Texas to move here. Why would you want to do that?"

I touch his forearm, wrapping my fingers around him and squeezing. My eyes moisten with tears. Hunter's not fooling me with his cool exterior. He's trying to protect himself. I get it, but he needs to understand how I feel.

"Because you're here, and I want to be with you." He steps back. My arm falls to my side. Without another word, he turns away from me. "I'm not leaving for good, Hunter. I'll be back soon."

Chapter Thirty-Six

Hunter

"What do you mean she just left?"

Kennedy looks back at me with sorrowful eyes. It's bad enough that I didn't catch on that *Uncle Tom* was involved in this. It's bad enough that I wasn't here to save them myself. I pushed Kate away. I should have said something. I should have told her that I love her. I should have kissed her. Anything would have been better than walking away from her. *Shit.*

"Did she say *when* she will be back?"

"No. She said that she was going out for a drive to think some things over." Kennedy's annoyance is clear. I have completely fucked up.

"Hunter, Kate's stuff is still here. She didn't even take a coat. She'll be back." I shrug my shoulders. "Have you tried to call her?"

"Several times. The calls go straight to voicemail."

"Hunter, she'll be back."

"When I talked to her this afternoon on the phone...it wasn't good." Then, later, I really messed things up.

"What did you do? Was it about the gray paint?"

I shake my head. "I didn't even know about the paint then. I was angry with her. I got on her about a couple things, but that wasn't what I was actually mad about. I was afraid that she would do exactly this—that she would leave. Then I only made it worse. Why didn't I just tell her how I feel about her? I sound like some kind of sappy loser."

"No. You sound like someone in love. She loves you, too."

"How do you know?"

"I just do. I think she's loved you for a long time."

"How can you say that? She's hated me for years."

"She came to see you after Mom passed away."

"What?" My brow furrows in disbelief. How could I not know that?

"Dad yelled at her, and she left."

"Why didn't she ever tell me?"

"Probably for the same reason I never did. Dad was in pretty bad shape that day. He was mean to her." *Katie.* "She'll be back."

Last time it took her ten years to come back to

me. How long will it take this time? One thing's for sure, that was only because fate intervened. If Kate doesn't come back this time, I'm going after her.

Chapter Thirty-Seven

Kate

Exhausted doesn't begin to describe how I feel as I drive through Davidson. Nervous and excited are also in the mix. My stomach was doing flips when I crossed into Virginia from Tennessee, but that was four hours ago. Now, I'm about to throw up.

I didn't plan what time I would arrive back at Hunter's. I just tried to get back here as soon as humanly possible. The last couple days are a blur. I guess I knew deep down what I was doing when I left Hunter's house the other day. I just hadn't let myself know all the details yet. I drove to Dulles and just made the last direct flight to Austin. That got me home at midnight. I was up early on Tuesday to do all the things I had to do. Pack the car. Call for reinforcements. Maddy and Josie had never seen me so determined. They're good friends, though, and they could tell how much this means to me. I was worn out when I fell into bed at six o'clock that evening, but I had everything either packed or tagged for giveaway or donation. Josie is going to handle the distribution.

I tried to sleep, and I did sleep until just after midnight. Then, visions of Hunter and the drive that lay ahead of me crept into my dreams. So, I was on the road by two am on Wednesday. I've had a twenty-one hour drive to contemplate my actions. I don't regret them...at all. Davidson is my home. Hunter is my home. I have to get back to him as soon as possible. Once everything with Brady and the diamond smuggling case was solved, I didn't want to waste any time.

Hunter is likely very angry with me right now. He called me five times on Monday. I didn't answer any of his calls. I sent Mom and Brady each a text once I arrived at Dulles to tell them that I would be in touch soon. A chicken move for sure, but once I'd made up my mind, I didn't want anything or anyone to get in my way.

The twenty-one hour car trip has given me lots of time to talk on the phone. I'm way over in my minutes this month. I've spoken with Brady the most. He's doing well considering, but his healing will take time. He's always been one of the most trusting people I know, but this whole Jamie thing may have ruined that.

Mom has called often to check on me. I haven't told her my plan. She will find out soon enough, and she'll be so happy she won't care that she is the last to know.

Kennedy is handling her situation remarkably well. She's such a strong young woman. Hunter made sure of that. He made sure that she can take care of herself, and she did. She took care of me, too. Now, I'm going to help take care of her. I always wanted a sister. Part of me was in such a hurry to get back here to Kennedy, too. It's not just Hunter—although he's the biggest part of it—it's everyone here who's such a big part of my life.

I turn slowly onto Hunter's driveway. It's going on eleven, and there's still light coming from some of the windows. *Thank you, God.* Things wouldn't be off to a great start if I had to wake him up.

There he is.

Hunter's standing at the door as I exit my car. His face is unreadable, but he most definitely isn't smiling.

Deep breath.

I take my time climbing onto the porch, steeling my nerves with each step. The air is cold, much colder than what I left in Texas. I'm used to it though. It's home.

"What are you doing here?"

I step close enough to Hunter to see his eyes.

They're his most expressive feature, so I need to be able to read him as best as I can.

"What do you mean? I said that I would be back soon."

He folds his arms carefully and hugs them to his chest. "Soon is a few minutes or a couple hours. You've been gone for days."

"Only two days. I had some stuff to do. Are you going to invite me inside? It's a long drive from Austin to Davidson."

"You drove? Why?"

"Because I can't fit everything I own into a suitcase. I fit what I could into my car and gave away everything else."

He studies me carefully. "Why would you do that?" The words are almost a whisper.

"Because this is my home, Hunter." His eyes widen. His nostrils flare with his quick intake of breath. *I just scared the crap out of him.* "I don't mean here exactly, but Davidson is my home. I tried to tell you, but you wouldn't believe me. So, I wanted to prove to you that I meant it."

"I didn't mean to be so rude to you then. I was scared. The people I love leave me."

"That's not true anymore. Your dad didn't leave you, and I'm not going anywhere."

Hunter pulls me to him until our chests touch, and we can't get any closer—at least with our clothes on. Our faces are only inches apart as his fingertips lightly brush my cheek.

"I've always loved you, Katie." I close my eyes and let his words flow through me.

"I love you, too, Hunter I'm sorry that it took me so long to figure it out."

His lips lightly touch my cheek. "Wait right here."

Hunter walks down the steps and opens the trunk of my car. He carries my suitcase and a large duffle bag back onto the porch.

"What are you doing?"

"I'm moving you in. This is where you belong, here with me. You can paint every wall and publish a book about it for all I care. Just stay with me. In fact." Hunter takes my hands in his and kneels down in front of me. "Marry me, Katie."

"Yes!" The word squeaks out as the tears start to roll. Hunter pulls me to him, and then his lips are on mine, warm and sure and perfect. *Just like home should be.*

Dear Reader,

I hope you enjoyed *Deciding Fate*. If so, please consider writing an online review. Reviews are very helpful and would be very much appreciated.

If you would like to be notified of upcoming releases, please sign up for my newsletter at www.tamralassiter.com. I'd also love to connect with you on Twitter or Facebook.

Sincerely,

Tamra Lassiter

Also by Tamra Lassiter

Other titles in the *Role of Fate* series:
Blinding Fate
Creating Fate

Romantic Suspense:
No More Regrets
Perfectly Innocent
Something to Lose
I Take Thee to Deceive
Favorable Consequences

Young Adult Fantasy:
The Gifted

Acknowledgements

Who would have guessed when I met Trinh in high school that we'd still be such great friends today? That was more than thirty years ago. So much has happened since then—college, marriage, children, raising the children. Yikes! So many good times and even some bad ones. She is patient, kind, and loyal and the best best friend a person could have. I wouldn't be the person I am today without her friendship.

Many thanks to my friends and family who are beta readers. Thanks to Suzanne Bhattacharya, Anne Newport, June Kuhne, Peggy Lassiter, and Pat Williams.

Special thanks to Mary McGahren for the incredible cover. You are truly amazing!

Thanks to Jena O'Connor of Practical Proofing, Toni Metcalf, and Mary Featherly for all your help with editing and proofing.

And last, but certainly not least, thank you to my loving husband and daughters for your unending support. You mean the world to me!

Made in the USA
Charleston, SC
14 March 2016